Jawa

CW00530827

Jaws of Death

Victoria Meye

Strategic Book Publishing
Vero Beach, Florida, USA
www.sbpra.net

For information about special discounts for bulk purchases, please contact Strategic Book Publishing, Special Sales, at bookorder@sbpra.net.

ISBN: 978-1-68235-838-2

What critics say about JAWS OF DEATH

"Jaws of Death" narrates the story of a young academician who lives behind her husband and son, and travels to the United States of America for an academic stint. Upon completion, she is caught on the horns of a dilemma whether to stay on and brave the vagaries of the complex US immigration system, or return to a place called home currently embroiled in an internecine war. Her love for family and country triumphs over any intentions to stay, and she returns home where she is inevitably captured in the throes of the "jaws of death". The story of how she untangles herself from the complex web is what unfolds in the "Jaws of Death".

The story is profoundly enthralling, as it is nerve-racking. While a piece of literary ingenuity, it draws from the ossified facts of the history of the aggrieved people of former British Southern Cameroons through the lens of a returning academician. She is not spared the excesses of the banana republic she is returning to, where the dissent is treated with brutal repression, wanton arrests and recklessly abandoned to death. The brilliance of the novel shines the author's ability to feed the mind with uncanny palpability; the ABCs of the historical aberration that led to the conflict in Cameroon as she faces the destiny of identifying the soul of the nation. The novel is an "unputdownable" piece, and reads like a beautiful symphony; the gory details notwithstanding. This is a must read piece.

Lambert Mbom, *Critical Thinker and Professional Journalist.*

Jaws of Death is not just metaphorically deep but represents a salient dimension in postcoloniality. It is a tale about the execution of the Ambazonia war, the causes, and by implicature, the story of the not-so-united Cameroon, casting a dark silhouette on the Anglophone minority war in Cameroon with a tonality that is profoundly riveting, revealing, and ridiculously breathtaking. The picture depicted is bleak, the torture deep, and survival is mere luck.

With a first-person narrative technique, the author through Matilda becomes the mouthpiece of the struggle, also using other victims to narrate their distinct and individual tragedies, as their spiritual essence in the liturgy of a survival in jail. Characters are as true to life as are the conflict scenarios with their crippling and gipping effects. It is not only a dramatic narrative sodden with suspense and expectation but a family saga of an expectant husband with his young son, waiting for his wife to arrive from abroad just to receive her call from jail. The emotional and psychological trauma so devastating, that, if literary writing were ever to address topicality, this would be it, especially with the war going on unabated. The story ends with His Majesty Yabi declaring the end of hostilities and releasing the prisoners of conscience. Whether such a scenario is feasible in real life remains to be seen.

JK Bannavti, Author: Leopard Watch,
Rock of God, and The Reapers & Freed into Jail

Dedication

To **Vitalis Bamngha Wolen** alias **Taylor** and **Pa Frederick Wirsiy** nicknamed **Le Vieux** *(by Soldiers);* the oldest in the detention camp in SED – *Gendarmerie Nationale.* These two and many others were arrested from different areas of Southern Cameroon in relation to the Anglophone crisis, and whisked to prisons in Yaoundé, Cameroon's capital, where they were tortured for months and died in detention without being tried. May the spilling of their blood find justice.

One thing you can't hide – is when you're crippled inside

John Lennon

CHAPTER ONE

I travelled to the U.S when the Anglophone saga, now a full-blown war, was in its early throes. Within nine months of my stay in America what began as a peaceful protest with fresh plants and branches took a nosedive for the worse. With an iron fist the military clamped down on the protesters, killing women, children, and the elderly. Hundreds were tortured and abandoned between the world of the living and that of the dead. Thousands were arrested and thrown in dungeons dotted across the country. A thousand more were forced to flee overnight to the bushes for fear of military incursions as helicopter gunships kept hovering over the Anglophone regions, especially in hot spot areas.

It was in the midst of these tumultuous and turbulent times that I outlived my academic stay in the U.S. and had to return to Cameroon. Not only were government officials grilling English-speaking Cameroonians at the airport, and going through their phones and computers, but they were also abducting most of them under the guise that they were those funding the separatist fighters and calling for an independent nation called Ambazonia. As an Anglophone, I suspected my case would be dicey at the airport because I had attended some meetings in Washington D.C. and in Bowie, Maryland that were organized by some of the separatist leaders.

Cold chills ran down my spine when my friends and colleagues informed me that there was a long list at the airports with names of people who attended any separatist meetings abroad. Thus, on the eve of my departure fear paralyzed me. I am not sure I could account for an hour's sleep that night. I was on the edge of the bed pestered by morbid thoughts the entire night. I missed my husband and son, Junior Konyuy, and was so eager to see them.

I was also excited to present a certificate of distinction to my husband and family as proof of my excellent performance at the program I had just completed in the U.S. I could recollect my uncle's prophetic words after my brilliant performance at the end of course certificate – Advance Level's results; when he suggested, "You will attain higher heights in academia; you will always be a trailblazer whatever enterprise you find yourself in. Go and conquer, my child." These prophetic words motivated me in life, and I was always determined to turn everything I touched into gold, especially to be the best in any program I enrolled in. These words of wisdom became clear the day I defended my Ph.D. with an outstanding score. I was glad my uncle was still alive to see his prophecy become reality. My mother shed tears of joy when well-known and highly distinguished professors placed the academic robe on me.

After graduation, I was immediately hired to teach History and International Relations in the University, and soon selected to take part in a UNESCO Academic and Cultural Exchange Program for three months in India. My performance in the program in India paved my way to being selected as one of ten participants in the exchange program for nine months in the U.S. There was consideration that I might be hired to work for UNESCO. This was going to be a good deal for my family and me. While waiting for this job consideration to go full-circle, I had to go back to Cameroon to continue working with my university. Had I stayed one more night in the U.S., I would be deported, and this would jeopardize my chances of ever going back again. Travelling to Cameroon was synonymous with walking into a trap with both eyes wide open.

In both meetings I attended in the U.S., I was at the fringes, and the gatherings were so crowded that I wondered whether any government agent spotted me. Cameroonian law is a jungle when it concerns the Anglophone Crisis. If I were to be bundled up and incarcerated, I would die of a skin disease, torture, or venereal disease from rape. "Oh God," I squeaked that night. It was such a long, long night for me. Worse, I had overheard that some of those nobbled at the airport were already facing military trials on secession charges. Death sentences were dangling over their heads like the sword of Damocles.

My chest stuttered and I wiped my eyes, which were beginning to pool as time dragged on. I did not want to die like a rat. Jails in that country are not what one would wish on one's worst enemy. It was my civic right to attend a rally. Oh, but exercising one's civic right was not in Cameroon's vocabulary. At one time I regretted that I had attended those rallies; at another time I convinced myself that I was a woman and would be treated with some mercy.

I could not count how many times that night I checked the time. I was nervous and edgy. Once it was past midnight, I started packing my handbag with items I needed handy just to while away time.

When it was finally dawn, I made the sign of the cross, hurriedly took a shower for the umpteenth time to face my destiny. Though I dreaded what awaited me in Cameroon, I also hoped luck would smile my way.

I closed my eyes and images of Junior and my darling husband danced on my face like flickering stars. My muscles quivered and I felt like exploding. I realized I'd not eaten even a morsel besides the cereal I had nibbled and a cup of milk I'd drunk in the morning. I pounded my fists against my thighs and stormed to the kitchen seething with rage. I made a sandwich, but the bland wheat bread tasted in my mouth like gravel. After struggling with the first bite, I cast it in the dustbin, sighed deeply, and tossed my phone to the far end of the carpet.

Before I could recollect what I had almost done with my phone, the door creaked open. Behold, it was the smiling face of Patrick, my cousin and host, exposing his gap-tooth and saying, "Sorry Sister, hope you'll not kill me today." He was such a dashing and dapper young man with cropped-up hair, rounded forehead, and drowsy eyes.

I gathered myself and drew in slow, steady breaths. "Patrick, we have just forty minutes left," I said, looking at my wristwatch.

"I had a hectic day at work," he said while still standing by the door.

"Show those dimples to those girls." I stood and shushed him with a wave.

In the car he began explaining to me about his frenetic day at the McDonald's where he worked and how he could not even check his phone, according to work policy, and how a cop stopped him on the way for speeding. I was too tense to respond to his tirade, and so we drove in silence. I was praying to the heavenly hosts for a miracle at the airport in Cameroon.

We got to the airport by 4:55pm. But before I could alight from his car, he sighed and said in a deep sorrowful voice, "Yaa is no more."

My heartbeat raced. "Yaa Shuka? Because she had been sick for a very long time now?"

Patrick kept quiet for one full minute and then said, "Yaa Bonglam."

My phone dropped to the floor of the car. During my primary school days, she often gave us *Tuhkuni* (mashed potatoes and beans) and at times sweet yams when we were returning from school. I felt guilty that I had not given her enough as I would have wished.

"Was she sick?"

"The military shot her around the Vekovi hill when she was returning from the farm."

I froze.

When I finally reached the receptionist and submitted my passport, the woman looked at it, manipulated the computer and growled like a gaunt dog, "Your name is not in the system." My every muscle tensed. I wished I could levitate.

"How?"

"I guess there's a mistake," she said, shrugging her shoulders.

"My name is Yenyuy Matilda," I huffed.

She smiled and said, "Sorry, I can't find it."

"But I paid for a round trip," I said and began rummaging my handbag. The people in the line, who were perhaps frustrated, began grumbling.

"Where are you going to?"

"Cameroon," I said.

"No flight leaves from here to Cameroon."

I raised my voice and waved my printed ticket. "Is this not my ticket?"

A police officer appeared and took me aside. When I explained everything to her, she said I had taken the wrong route and was on the wrong lane. She said I was supposed to stop at Paris before boarding another plane to Yaoundé, which she pronounced Yondeh. She then took me all the way from the lobby to another section of the building. The time was already 5:10pm. Tears pooled in my eyes as we arrived at the new checkpoint. One old and tired white man was checking in.

The receptionist checked my documents, gave me a broad and contagious smile, and said, "You're damn lucky, Ma'am. If not for a thirty-minute delay, you would have missed your flight."

I was directed to take my luggage to one compartment for weighing. After weighing the bags, the attendant told me that my luggage was ten pounds more than the required travelling weight.

While I was contemplating what to take out, his supervisor came and told him to be fast. Before he could explain anything, another boss called him. The supervisor hurriedly threw my luggage on the conveyor and told me to take the elevator two levels down. He directed me where to take the monorail, which was to take me to my gate to board the plane.

Smashing toes and saying "ashia" as if I was in Cameroon pleading for a wrong done, I got to the area allocated for me. The slurs hurled at me glided like dew on leaves. When I plodded to my seat on the plane, I flopped in it like human dung. The passengers had fastened their seatbelts, ready for takeoff. I was extremely tired and hungry. I reached out for some honey bunch biscuits in my handbag and threw a piece in my parched mouth and began munching. I then reclined my seat and leaned backwards. Only one thing was on my mind—Junior, the light of my life.

CHAPTER TWO

When I snuggled my head closer to the cushion, it immediately had a soporific effect. By the time the hostess was dishing out her rant about safety and what to do during an emergency I was listening as if from another planet. The humdrum talk lulled me further, as if she was singing a lullaby. I found myself floating on the firmament. I'm sure this happened so fast because of my hectic day and my unusual excitement and anxiety.

When I dozed off, I saw myself in a reverie at the Nsimalen International Airport in Yaoundé. Contrary to expectations, I passed through the different gates at the airport so easily and quickly like a V.I.P. From afar I could see my husband, Junior, and some family members looking aghast as if I would not come. Just when I was wondering why they were sad, I woke up from the dream; hagridden.

The death of Yaa Bonglam began to haunt me. What was the rationale for killing the old woman? She had no idea what the war was all about, yet she had been murdered in cold blood. A week ago, my husband had told me that Pa Tukov and his donkey were shot by stray bullets at Wainamah. Yaa Wirntem had gone the same way. "May your gentle soul be wrapped in God's fur," I squeaked, wiping my eyes.

A hostess nudged my shoulder. My nose was assailed by some spicy food. She was holding a plate of macaroni and cheese with broccoli and a glass of chilled wine.

I yawned, rubbed my eyes, and looked at the time. We have been flying for more than three hours. When it dawned on me that I had been dreaming, I chewed on my bottom lip. Hunger had begun gnawing at the walls of my intestines. When I tasted the food, I felt a tang on my tongue and grimaced. It was too spicy. However, I ravenously ate the food with the appetite of an anaconda. I then nursed the wine while rehearsing how I was going to behave at the airport. *"Who wants to try me?"* I giggled and muttered to myself before realizing that I was in an uncomfortable environment for such sassiness.

I glazed over the edges of my long and graceful hair while using a portable mirror; I freshened up my lips by holding them inwards, and smiled, exposing the dimples on my chubby cheeks. I imagined myself holding my suitcase containing my laptop and descending from the plane like the first lady. Thoughts of how I was going to be courtly as I walked off the plane while waving at the crowd of relations, friends, and students that would come to welcome me, exactly the way the president's luscious and glamorous wife used to do, inundated my crowded mind. As these thoughts pestered me, I swilled the wine, and asked for more.

When I had drunk two glasses, my head started pounding and reeling. Everywhere on the plane seemed giddy. I got up to use the rest room but sank back on my seat, utterly woozy. After waiting for about thirty minutes, I mustered strength, held the bars on the plane and wobbled to the restroom. There, I thrusted my finger in my throat and regurgitated everything. I felt some relief when I returned to my seat.

After about an hour and thirty minutes, the hostess passed around again with food. I served myself some seafood and some noodles. The food was so delicious that I savored with a gargantuan appetite and regretted why I did not take as much. When one of the hostesses came for the disposable dishes, the plane galloped, she tripped and tumbled on me. The mess from the plate smeared my sexy pink T-shirt with white stripes around my chest.

This was an unfortunate incident because my dresses were in my luggage. My mind was focused on getting to Charles de Gaulle Airport fast so that I could get another dress on transit. When we got to Paris, I was informed that my luggage went on a cargo plane, and I should expect to receive that as soon as I get to Cameroon. Though I had tried to clean the splotches where the mess dropped, the black skirt still looked disheveled. We had just an hour and a half to board the next plane. I decided to look for where clothes were sold. I knew they were going to be at cut-throat prices, but I had no choice.

After wondering around, I saw one place with trendy clothes for both women and men. It was only when I saw the prices on the goods in Euros that I remembered I had but dollars on me meant to send my admirers awestruck. I decided to first look for where I could change the dollars to Euros.

When I succeeded and came back to the shop, I saw a pair of jeans and my mind went back to the dream I'd had on the plane. I scrutinized the blue elastic jeans and concluded they would fit me well. I needed a T-shirt that would match. Fortunately, I got one. It was white with a crescent conspicuous writing on its front: Winners Never Quit. Underneath the writing was the picture of a hand firmly closed. I went in for the jean pants and the T-shirt after measuring them. Directly opposite the shop, was a stall for selling shoes. I bought some tennis shoes that could match the outfit. I came back to the shop and bought a fez hat bearing the likeness Barack Obama. I also purchased some shirts for my husband and a pair of shoes for Junior.

I felt elated in my new outfit. I swaggered to where I was to board the next plane full of airs. It was there that I realized that

I had to go through some transit rituals. This time around, I was lucky, and things moved so fast.

When I got on the plane, someone was sitting on my allocated seat. The seat was beside the window, and I could not trade it for anything. I wanted to sit there so that I could get an aerial view of Paris and Yaoundé, take pictures and video footages. When I stood by her thinking she would leave politely, she wouldn't budge; I showed her my air ticket and pointed to her my seat number. She spoke to me in French that it was her right to sit anywhere. Even though I could speak French, I chose to speak in English.

"Please can I sit in seat that matches my ticket?" I asked calmly.

"You Anglophones, who do you think you are!" she screamed. Then she tapped her butt. "Or is it because of your broad hips?"

"Madam, this has nothing to do with Anglophones and body-build here."

"I came here first," she insisted.

"It doesn't matter," I said and then added, "What counts is the seat number on your ticket."

From her accent I could decipher she was a Beti lady—born and breed in Yaoundé. My mind went to the Anglophone problem that was turning the country topsy-turvy. Her action had created a scene because the people on the plane were looking at us in disbelief.

With a pained stare, I said, "If you don't leave, I will report to the flight attendants."

She clapped her hands, cachinnated derisively and burst: "*Eekieh*, Anglofool…break the sky, I will not leave from this place."

"A wry smile danced on my forehead. Why do you think that Anglophones don't have rights?"

"Leave me alone," she retorted and planted her jaw by the side of the plane.

Her action pierced my heart like rusted spikes as I battled the urge to recoil. I thought of lifting her from the seat, but my civility would not permit me. My somewhat boisterous life in my secondary school days had completely left me.

"Go to Bamenda, and do whatever you want," she said and emphasized, "This is Camairco."

I felt slighted by her words and my mood plummeted. I went for the flight attendant who immediately came and told her to sit in her rightful place. She shamefully left threatening to teach me a lesson when we got to Yaoundé. I curled my shoulders over my chest wondering how people could be so mean. She thought that everywhere was a jungle.

When I settled in my rightful seat, I nodded my head like Chinua Achebe's lizard after accomplishing a task as I glowed inside. Though I felt a pain in the back of my throat, I was smug for standing my grounds. I had encountered situations in Yaoundé where Anglophones were made to play second fiddle and where a stark illiterate Francophone saw himself more elevated than an Anglophone professor. The practice had gone on for more than six decades and had almost become the norm. It was this kind of back-seat position for more than half a century that had caused English-speaking Cameroonians to begin protesting.

While in the U.S, I had attended a couple of meetings in solidarity with my Anglophone brethren in the Diaspora who were trying to chart the way forward to be free from the shackles of Francophone marginalization, exploitation, and oppression. The Anglophone palaver had gained steam and there was no turning back. I wondered what the woman could do to me. After thinking about the plight of Anglophones in Cameroon for a while, I decided to shove the thought aside even though it kept rearing its ugly head.

An inner wave of happiness continued to emanate from within me and radiate to my face. In less than five hours, I would be in the warmth and comfort of my family. I wetted my lips, checked my phone, and realized that my husband had sent me a couple of WhatsApp messages. Elation suffused my being. He said Junior was fine and asleep, and that almost all his colleagues were to be at the airport. He also stated that he had booked a hall in town for a welcome party that same evening. He wrote that even if I were so tired, my shadow would represent me at the party. The waiting will soon be over, and in our usual romantic joking style; he insisted that *ngwan-ngwan* was not going to be easy. Underneath the messages were a bouquet of flowers and red heart sign.

My hopes of a better life were rekindled. I clasped my hands to my chest and began jittering my feet against the floor. I clenched my lips and pinned my fingers and toes for the pilot to apply jet-plane speed from Paris to Yaoundé. Unlike the pizzas, the Popeye's, and the McDonald's, I will savor *tuhkuni* aplenty again. I wished I had come with an MP3 player I would have been listening to Richard Kings latest hit. I was anxious, and a sense of foreboding doom and gloom hovered around me.

CHAPTER THREE

When the plane took off for Yaoundé, I gave a darting gaze to the firmament and passengers. I thought of the woman's queer behavior, which was symptomatic of the maltreatment meted on Anglophones in Cameroon, and as I looked at her with utter profanity, my eyes appeared flat, excessive saliva filled in my mouth, and was nauseated at her ugly mannerism. There was nothing I could do other than flinch in disgust. English-speaking Cameroonians have played second fiddle despite their natural resources, capabilities, and high literacy. I debated on the mayhem currently going on in the country and pressed my knees together. Since those thoughts were dampening, I forced myself to think about my reception at the airport and how many family members and friends were surely warming up to welcome me with ululation. Wiggling my waist, I crossed and uncrossed my legs despite the little space.

I gloried in the red-carpet reception in my hallucinations for a while until it lulled me to a nap. I was soon awakened by jerks and bumps that scared the hell out of me. I felt as if my insides were quivering when I woke up and heard the engine of the plane sounding like a rusted car out of gas while the driver was struggling to trundle a steep hill. One of the hosts was explaining something which I did not fully understand. My chest tightened and my breathing accelerated. Every passenger was alert.

All I could remember was that I saw some passengers putting on oxygen masks while screaming "Jesus . . . Jesus . . . Jesus . . ." and beckoning on God to intervene. My face turned ashen. Others were screaming in different languages and calling on their ancestors to help. I kept chewing the inside of my left cheek after I had opened my mouth to call on Mary the Mother of Jesus and it hung open. Although, the situation lasted for less than two minutes, I saw what people would do in a near death situation. I had just remained glued to my seat; too dazed to act. I was thinking of my family, my earthly exploits, and plans to paint Yaoundé red—how all would have gone to ruins in the split of a second had things gone wrong. I started talking to myself with assurances that I shall live and not die. Amidst the chaos on board the plane, One of the plane waiters kept assuring us that all would be well, and that the pilot was trying hard to regulate the situation. A whisk of a smile hovered over my face and disappeared instantly.

In that brief interval, life narrowed before me to a dot and then vanished. I was jerking back and forth on my seat. I made my last prayer calling on God to forgive my sins and to take care of my family, especially Junior, once I was gone—never to be seen again. I knew that the plane would plummet into the Atlantic Ocean or one dense forest where our remains would forever be out of sight. I tried to peep through the window but saw thick grey fog hovering below the plane. My lips began moving slowly as words refused to form. I clasped my right hand over my mouth and gripped the side of my seat.

When the plane's movement finally stabilized, we all erupted into ululations, guffaws, and discordant clapping, pouring praises upon praises on to the pilot. This happened so spontaneously. It took a while for me to come back to normalcy. My heartbeat spasmodically for quite some time before it normalized. Happiness sparkled inside me.

Aside the technical fault, the rest of the journey was uneventful. I ate very little and was in pensive mood throughout. My eyes were gritty for want of sufficient sleep, but I was ready to brave it. I did not want to miss any unforeseen again. Occasionally, I would doze off and get up with jetlag feelings.

About thirty minutes for the plane to land, a waiter told us to remember to get our belongings once the plane landed. I could feel the plane lowering from its altitude. The clouds gave way to rivers, hills, and dense forests. Afterward, I began seeing houses though they looked like tiny particles. At last, the houses were clearer. I could identify some conspicuous structures like the ministerial complexes, Hilton hotel in downtown Yaoundé, the Ahmadou Ahidjo Stadium, and the Bank of Central African States. Lower and lower, the plane came down like a swallow during one of its mesmerizing antics.

I could not believe my eyes. My heart jumped to my palms. Doused in sweat, I dabbed my face with a tissue. At last, I was back to my beloved country torn by dissension, disillusionment, corruption, and marginalization—the heart of prebendalism in Africa, and the most corrupt country in the world for two consecutive years. When the plane finally touched on the tarmac, I began humming. Not even a nightingale was a match. The passengers' faces were beaming with joy as they burst into thunderous handclapping hailing the pilot as their hero. I joined the bandwagon as my eyes sparkled. Everyone wanted to see the great pilot who brought a near disaster under control, saving hundreds of lives.

While the passengers were struggling to catch a glimpse of the pilot who had suddenly become an enigma, I went straight to the restroom with my handbag containing my one-stop make-up box to give a last touch to my face. My hands trembled as I held the mirror and tried to apply my red lipstick. The foundation on my face had begun to wear out. I gave it a face-lift. When I was done with my eyelashes and eyelids, I carefully applied some hand lotion. I ended the beauty show by putting on a seductive perfume with a pungent, yet attractive aroma that I bought in a mall at Ocean City in Maryland. Two puffs of breath spray in my mouth echoed the words "good to go" in my ears.

I was almost the last person to leave the plane. Immediately I stepped out the humid atmosphere was stifling. I had to take a few steps backwards to prepare myself for the sudden change of climate.

I could see some of the passengers I had boarded the plane with trekking from the large expanse of where the plane had landed to be checked before going for their luggage. Relatives and friends were at the lobby constructed like a balcony and protected by transparent glass. I wondered what my family and friends would be thinking about since they had not seen me yet. Though the lobby was about a hundred meters away from where the plane landed, I could see my husband who had carried Junior with one hand and waving at me with the other hand. My heart melted.

Though the sky was clear when the plane was about to land, things took a curveball in minutes. The skies suddenly turned grey as if the devil was about to smite the nation. Before I could come out of the plane, the second time, mother earth had unleashed its tantrums and in one gush, the grey skies went mad, pouring heavily like a devil emptying its bladder.

It was an opportunity for the young, the old, the less important and the VIP to prove that they have been taking their sports or P.E classes seriously. One thing that strokes me was that the thunderstorm did not distinguish who was low and who was great. Everyone had one goal—to run to shelter. As we displayed our agility while the rains pelted us for close to five minutes since the lobby was meters away, those who had gathered at the lobby were jeering and some were making catcalls.

I ran so fast since I was putting on a pair of jean pants and sporting shoes. Unfortunately, when I was about to jump to the veranda of the building, my handbag dropped spilling its content. It was in the course of gathering the stuff that fell from the handbag that the waters from above dealt a big blow on the make-up I had painstakingly done to look smart and dashing.

I treaded to the first checkout point head bowed and with my matted hair like a mouse soaked in palm oil. My lips chattered and I shivered as if I had suffered a bout of relapsing fever.

CHAPTER FOUR

When I rushed to the checkout point though still wet and unkempt, I was nervous. I just wanted to see my family, and so had no time for any make-up or for any courtly show. My wetness and anxiety built in me some lion courage, and I threw caution to the wind; stepping on toes and jostling this or that person just to edge my way in front. I believed my bravado and feminine sex gave me the aptitude to be eight on the line. The line moved faster than expected, and in less than no time, I had just two persons ahead of me since everything moved like goods in a conveyor belt.

One of the two persons ahead of me was a white woman. When it was her turn, the Immigration and Customs Agents did not bother her for a second. When she attempted to pull out her documents to show the officers, they waved her reverentially to move on. Next was the person before me. He was a young black man. When he showed his passport, one of the officers shoved it aside grumbling something like "We need to watch out for you people from Britain and America." The officer cornered his colleague and they whispered to each other, and the officer asked the man to open his suitcase. He was a well-groomed man. He had a diamond watch glittering on his wrist, as his hands trembled to flip-open his suitcase.

I looked at my watch in anxiety as the Immigration control pace seemed to slow down, and in frustration, stamped my feet on the rough and dirty floor. I just could not bear wasting any second in that humid dungeon of an airport. I felt like bypassing the Immigration and Customs Agents and get to my family. I had arrived and beauty would not keep me from meeting my loved ones in all gaiety. At least they saw the tempestuous storm and my travails. The fact that God brought me safely was a testimony.

When one of the officers asked the young man in front of me if he was called Larry Tumenta, and he replied in the affirmation, the officer gave his passport to his colleagues. Larry had tucked in his sky-blue shirt over a spotless pair of black pants. They checked on a computer placed on a table in front of them and nodded their heads as if they were impressed by him. One of them said, "You are those living in your comfort zones abroad and causing all the confusion back here."

"This country is at the brink of war because of you people," one said. "Secessionists, terrorists."

"Please, can you explain what you said?" I heard Larry say confidently.

"We are not here in Britain," one of the officers said. "Take off those glasses before I break them."

He took off his glasses, and I saw what it meant to be suave and savvy. "Then can you return my passport to me?"

"This is not in our capacity to decide," the officer said.

"What wrong have I done?" Larry shook his head as he spoke.

The officer puffed out his chest. "You will soon know, terrorist."

Larry laughed drily and stopped abruptly. "I don't understand you," he said. He had such a refined accent and a manner of speaking the Queen's language that made me love listening to him.

"These are the people who sit back and destabilize the nation," the officer pointed to Larry as he explained to his colleague who just came in.

I adjusted my legs several times due to anxiety and the accusations heaped on poor Larry. I wondered what was going on through his mind. It could be so frustrating and harrowing. Perhaps his fiancée or wife or family members were anxiously waiting for him to present all the "goodies" from the white man's land, but here he was, accused of terrorism and secession. I just could not fathom what terrorist acts a dashing and apparently innocent young man like Larry could be involved in.

To cut the story short, one of the police officers made a phone call and within minutes, Larry was held by the collars of his shirt by two uniformed officers like a riff raff, handcuffed, and whisked off to an unknown destination. Rage bottled up within me, and I wished I were invisible to have dealt the heartless fellows some lethal blows.

When Larry was literally dragged away like an obstinate ass, one of the officers motioned to me to move forward; an alarm rang in my mind. I treaded ahead like a sheep going to the slaughter. I had begun to feel this strange premonition as bile kept rising from my stomach to my esophagus.

I presented my yellow fever card to the health officer in charge, and she said it was okay. Then I moved excitedly to the immigration officer and presented my passport. Suddenly he asked, "Where is the custom's form?" I responded, "I did not fill out the form as I thought it was meant for visitors." He showed it to me saying, "You must fill out this form". My temples began vibrating. It was then that I remembered seeing my next neighbor with it when the plane had landed, and she had said the forms were shared out when I was asleep. I had said to myself that if it were important, they would have given me. I had taken it for granted that it is my country, and it would not be necessary. I read my neighbor's own and saw questions like "What are you coming to do in Cameroon". "Where will you be living?" If in a hotel specify, "Which places do you intend to visit?" and others which to me were not meant for me since that was my country.

The impatient police officer asked me to step out of the line as I tried to ask another question. People behind me were already agitating, I guess because I was taking time. I had to go back to fill out the form before queuing up again. I felt sad, as I was to be the last on the line. It was a bitter pill to swallow given my anxiety, but I had to take it. I then collected the form from one officer and stepped out of the line to fill it out. I did it peacefully and came back to the line.

The line moved fast until I came in front of the police officer. All seemed okay as he stamped my passport, saying, "Madame go and get your luggage and you will get your passport at the exit after the custom check." I accepted and left him. At this time, nothing mattered to me than to get my luggage and meet my family that I knew was waiting for me anxiously at the waiting room. I then went to check my luggage, which was already passing on the luggage carousel, with people collecting theirs.

After thirty minutes, the same bags were passing, and after two rounds the baggage carousel stopped and someone collected the remaining bags. I shouted out, "Where is my luggage?" A worker in uniform immediately replied, "If you have not seen them passing it means your bags have not come." I could not believe what my ears heard. I told myself that maybe I did not understand French again. Then I composed myself, and asked him the procedure to recover my bags, and he asked me to follow him to an adjacent office.

When I entered this office, I saw two men one talking on his phone and the other playing a game on his tablet. I greeted them and said, "I have just come in through Camairco, and could not find my luggage." The man playing a game asked me where I had come from, at which I told him. Then he gave me a form to fill out for him to trace my bags.

The man took down my identification details including my telephone number to get to me when the luggage did finally come. I then left this office with a heavy heart but happy that I was finally home and would meet my husband and son at the waiting room after collecting my passport.

As I opened the door to the corridor, two police officers looking so uncompromising were already waiting at the entrance. They waved my passport to my face and asked me to follow them. I took two steps as my eyes bulged. Though taken aback, I mustered courage to ask them where they were taking me. One retorted without looking at me, "Just follow us, and stop asking questions." I took in a deep breath as my blood congealed. I trailed behind them like a house fly behind a pungent smell until we arrived at another room in the terminal building.

On our way, I saw my husband through the mirror playing with our baby. When I spotted them, instinctively I tried to wave but none of them saw me. My husband who was dressed in a Mitterrand blue shirt over a coffee pair of trousers and black pair of shoes was looking anxious. He would hold Junior's hand, leave it, pace up and down, and look around.

My anxiety reached fever peak, and I bumped into someone. He pushed me and shouted if I was all right. I saw my baby running around happily, and I was wondering if he knew where he was and what he had come to do there. I recalled how when I used to come back from the school where I taught; he would melt in my hands and would not want anyone to carry him, not even his father.

During those moments, I would be cooking with him on my back and singing lullabies to lull him to sleep. I would move around with him remembering those difficult five years of marriage without a child. Some of my in-laws had accused me then of being barren, but my husband stood by me.

When we got to the stuffy room full of files in cabinets and books strewn on the squalid floor, the officers banged the door behind them and motioned a threadbare seat for me to sit on. I hesitated, but the look on their faces made my feet buckle. The pendulum of an antic clock swung on the wall like a bell tolling the demise of a prominent religious personality. One of the men held my hand to stand. The other frisked me. It was strange indeed for two men and a woman locked up in a room under closed doors. I wondered whether they were really out to check me for hidden weapons, drugs, and other items because they concentrated on my breasts, thighs, and buttocks.

"Do you have a phone and or a computer?" one of them asked. I nodded.

He pointed to the table. "Put them here"

The items were in my hand luggage. I resisted thinking that they were simply trying to intimidate me so I could give a bribe, since the country was notorious for this unhealthy practice.

"Put the phone and computer here," the other officer thundered.

I was in a dilemma and clutched to the bag.

"Madam!" he screamed.

The baritone scared me, and I almost fell from the chair to the floor. With trembling hands, I handed my backpack to him. He took out my computer and telephone before throwing the bag at me.

"Are these the only gadgets you have?'

"Yes, Sir . . . oh yes please . . ."

"Are you deaf?"

I have another phone which have not been used."

He wrenched the bag from my trembling hands, took out the phone and thrusted it in one of the pockets on his jacket. I bade farewell to the brand-new Samsung Galaxy 8 I had bought for my husband worth hundreds of thousands of francs CFA.

He shoved the computer in front of me and asked me to turn it on. My picture server frightened the hell out of him. It was the picture of a man about thirty with a clean bullet hole drilled neatly on his forehead. He was stripped naked, and his genitals covered with a leafy branch. The incident occurred two days before my departure. It had happened in the Southern Zone in the town of Buea. The victim was on his way to the farm when the soldiers ended his life prematurely.

The man in uniform opened his eyes widely and exclaimed, *"Ambazonie, chien."* I could sense shame on the faces of the officers because they scratched their heads while one adjusted his belt repeatedly. He rummaged through the laptop nodding his head all the time. He then switched to my phone. I had attended some rallies in the U.S held by Southern Cameroonians to raise money to help the refugees languishing in Nigeria, and the internally displaced struggling for survival in the streets and bushes.

WhatsApp pictures and videos were their first stop. They combed through all my pictures, videos, and WhatsApp chats, nodding and talking to each other as they did that. My husband and a couple of friends have been updating me daily on the happenings back home. My phone contained horrific pictures and videos of the barbaric acts of the militia shooting people, torturing some, and burning houses. The modus operandi of Cameroonian soldiers was that anyone whose phone or laptop contained videos, pictures, or stories about the Anglophone crisis, no matter how remote the information, was an accomplice and as such a persona non grata. I could sense that my doom was near. My legs began dancing and I clasp the chair.

They went to my Facebook page. It was fraught with more dehumanizing brutal killings and clearing of crops, burning of foodstuff, and the killing of animals. Maimed corpses tortured and shot by soldiers were creepy even to the most daring. The officers winced as they caught site of the ghoulish sites.

I began breathing heavily. My legs trembled and I shuffled them to regain control. I changed position and gripped the table with my shaky hands. My end was nigh. Bile gushed out of my guts and scorched my throat. I tried to plead but realized that my tongue was stuck to the rough of my dry mouth. My eyes darted from the officers to the guns on their waists and to the picture on the wall of the head of state taken in his forties. Now he was stoop by age but still clung to power.

I placed my hands on the table pleading causing more harm as I mistakenly brought a pile of files crumbling down. A dirty slap welcomed me, and I went blank not knowing when my face had been buried among the scattered papers on the table. Stars dangled before my closed eyes, and I was nauseated.

"Raise your head," A voice bellowed.

I attempted to but failed. A slap on the back of my neck sent me scampering on the floor.

"Get up before I kill you."

A wave of revulsion and apprehension swept through me. "I am sorry . . . Have mercy on me . . . It's a mistake . . . Officers I don't know anything . . ."

"I say get up, terrorist."

When I raised my head, I squinted with what I saw. One of the officers was about landing a truncheon on my skull.

My face was all splotchy and I was still jolting from the impact of the slaps. "Please, don't kill me."

"You take these types of pictures and videos to sully the image of the supreme head of state and the country," he barked. "This cannot be tolerated, and you shall face the consequences."

All my hopes were dashed as I sat looking at places like a rat in the hands of a cat in an empty room. I was choking with anger. My frustration was total. The hopes of meeting my family were ebbing. The fanfare and the hopes of flaunting my discoveries all dashed. Wincing, I lifted my hands as if offering a prayer.

One of them guffawed curiously and shrugged his shoulders. "There is no God here, Madam Ambazonie."

They told me to follow them through a back door, I did not notice, to a waiting van. My hair bobbed and tears gushed out of my eyes. "Please, Sirs."

"Do not waste our time, woman."

I was just wondering what was in my husband's mind and the people gathered to hail me. My husband might have tried my number to no avail especially now that it was switched off.

None of them was moved by the fountain of tears pumping out of my eyes. Rather, the heartless men who thrived on schadenfreude were seized by a spooky laughter. Then a litany of taunts followed: "You cannot separate this country . . . Why have a beautiful woman like you joined such devilish group . . . You'll die in prison."

On the van, I was wedged between the officers who were too serious and alert to my liking. Where to? I knew not.

CHAPTER FIVE

When Larry was hauled to the van after a scuffle and the door banged against us, any lingering hope I had of meeting my family vanished. I felt my body simmering from the heat generated in the van. A stale smell wafted into my nostrils making the situation so uncomfortable. I just wondered if I would make it alive to wherever they were taking us. At least so that my family can see my remains. I just could not believe that I had actually come home to my family, which I had missed for months, only to be treated with spite. The trumped-up charges against me as a secessionist were alarming.

Larry was forced to sit between two police officers since one of those who sandwiched me jumped behind to accompany his colleague to protect Larry from escaping. He was doodling with a black pen shorter than a crayon. His left eye and jaw were swollen, and he tried as much as possible to maintain some equanimity though he occasionally winced as if in excruciating pain. Why they thought he could escape set my reason ablaze given that the doors to the van were fully sealed. In addition, he was handcuffed.

I turned and looked at him in the semi-dark van after it had driven for about five minutes. He seemed resigned to fate. Odium charged my being like electricity. Even when he was seemingly calm and ready to cooperate, the two officers still pinned his feet with their boots. One of the police officers wanted to hood him but his colleague nudged him not to.

I bowed my head to pray but only discordant sounds kept ringing in my ears as if I had suffered spells of tinnitus. In my mind's eye, I could see my family still waiting anxiously and hoping that I would soon appear to them like some comet. All passengers who had boarded that plane must have left and were surely in the comfort of their homes. Rage swept over me, and I balled my hands.

I could imagine my husband wondering if I was actually the person he had seen or was it my doppelganger. I pictured him tapping his skull and whispering to himself wondering if he was hallucinating. That was typical of him. I could see him not knowing what to tell little Junior. In addition, the rest of the family members and friends crestfallen and scratching their heads. Beads of tears rolled down my cheeks to my t-shirt. I had no strength to wipe the salty liquid.

Even though I was apprehensive, I still thought a miracle could happen at the last minute. It was like mourners hoping that their deceased would resurrect until the coffin was finally lowered into the bowels of the earth and covered with earth. The military van in front, whose siren had continued to inundate the vicinity, took the lead. An army jeep trailed behind us as if it was commissioned for a firing squad. As the van glided out of the precincts of the airport, it seemed it was my own Calvary odyssey.

My bleary vision could barely see outside since it was getting dark, and glasses of the van were tainted. I could imagine what others would be thinking when they saw the charade – siren blaring, light blinking. Some would think that some hardened criminals about to topple the regime had been captured in guerrilla warfare or some Boko Haram terrorists had been apprehended. As the van galloped on the bumpy and meandering Yaoundé tarmac amidst the deafening sound, I could feel my buttocks on the rugged tanned metal seat.

"If we don't teach these beasts a lesson, they would ruin the country," the military driver said.

"I least expected women to be involved in these secessionist and terrorist activities," my guard said.

"Hmm those you should fear most are women," the driver affirmed.

"But this lady does not appear devilish."

"What are you saying?" One of the officers in charge of Larry whistled. "These are the people you should dread."

"After the first baptism at the station, they will tell us the truth," the driver said.

I was frozen.

"I don't know why they should be wasting time," Larry's guard said. General Melinki's proposal was the best—"

"That we kill all suspects coming from abroad," Larry's guard said.

I uncontrollably wetted my underwear hearing that, and my soul jumped out of my body.

"Maybe if we do what Americans did in Hiroshima in some restive areas like Lebialem, Mamfe, Belo, Batibo, and Baghdad, then these Anglofools would fear and respect us," the driver said.

"You mean Kumbo where that daring parliamentarian comes from?"

"Yes, those animals call it Bagdad."

"It should be bombed first."

This pierced my heart like the sting of a black cobra since my husband's maternal grandmother came from this area. Something in me told me to speak up, but another voice told me to be calm. However, when the police officers continued to speak so disparagingly about Anglophones calling them animals, fools, and enemies in the house that deserved to be exterminated like cockroaches, I could no longer feign indifference. All along

29

Larry had been breathing heavily and occasionally clearing his throat each time something bad was said about Anglophones. His little pen was in his hand. I planned to ask him if it was a toy or some form of therapy when the opportunity arose.

"Are you really human?" I mustered courage and asked.

"Shut up woman," Larry's guard shouted.

"Look at what you are doing to us, innocent people."

"No Anglophone is innocent," the driver said.

"What have Anglophones done?" I asked.

Each of them tried to talk but had nothing to even rant. That was when I explained the genesis of the problem to them how West Cameroon and East Cameroon came together under the banner of unification with equal status, but things turned sour in the sham 1961 plebiscite.

Surprisingly, they gave a listening ear. I told them in French a brief history of Cameroon. It was the first day they were hearing that we had our independence in October 1, 1961, when the two regions formed The Federal Republic of Cameroon. I reminded them of the two stars on the flag representing the two nations and how La République had stealthily breached the constitution and singlehandedly changed the name from The Federal Republic of Cameroun to The United Republic of Cameroun and finally to The Republic of Cameroun with the two stars infused into one. By that, going against Article 47 of the constitution of the Federal Republic of Cameroon which stated that the form of state could not be changed. The president was to be the number one person in the country followed by the Vice President who was to be English speaking Cameroonian. See for yourselves how the State protocol is now: President of the Republic, President of the Senate, Speaker of the National Assembly, and President of the Economic and Social Council are all French speaking Cameroonian, Prime Minister- English speaking, President of the Constitutional Council – French speaking, President of the Supreme Court – French speaking and the list can go on and on with French speaking Cameroonians heading important state offices.

I could see the men yawning and scratching their heads as I schooled them. They even asked some questions, and both Larry and I clarified them. Since the atmosphere was somehow relaxed, Larry asked them why the wanton arrests, torture, and killings of Anglophone Cameroonians, and they said they were obeying orders from above.

"Hierarchy, hierarchy," I muttered.

Larry brought them to reason as he painstakingly explained the heydays of the West Cameroon economy, and how La République had inch by inch carted away or destroyed everything pertaining to Anglophones. Larry seemed so versed with the economy of West Cameroon prior to unification that I forgot my woes and listened attentively to the lecture he presented so eloquently. He spoke about the Cameroon Bank, WADA, UNVDA, POWERCAM, PWD, MIDENO, MIDEVIV and other state-owned corporations that made West Cameroon an envy to its La République counterpart. He mesmerized the officers with his eloquence in the French language that the officers decided to take him off the cuffs and promised to do so only when they arrived as to give their superiors the impression that he had been handcuffed all along.

Larry ended his lecture by talking about the much-cherished Anglo-Saxon educational system practiced in West Cameroon which La République wanted to annihilate. He showed them how the Anglophone system of education was preparing people for the job market and helping them to fish for themselves, which was a direct antipodal to the French system of education which prepared graduates to depend on the state for employment.

"You can give evidence that our schools are overpopulated with Francophones as testimony that our system of education is better off," he concluded.

Spontaneously they clapped. The driver could not be indifferent. I tilted my head to see the same vocal police officer who wanted to hood him tapping Larry's back and saying repeatedly, *"Non, vous avez raison."* He continued to say Anglophones were right to protest. He blamed the Francophones for being too indolent like sleeping sheep. One of the soldiers remarked, *"Les Anglophones sont bilingues"*. This was proof that Larry and I had eloquently educated them about our history in their language – French.

As the van wheeled through the main entrance to the police station, the officer hurriedly slipped the handcuffs into Larry's wrists. When it was about screeching to a halt, I could perceive the silhouettes of the soldiers who trailed behind us as they jumped out of their vans with their guns pointing to our van. One of the soldiers pulled open the door and the police officer sitting next to me helped me get down the van. When I alighted out of the van, Larry followed suit. We were guided to the police station like hardened criminals to the guillotine.

CHAPTER SIX

When we arrived at this station, I was asked to sit down on a wooden chair in one tight and stuffy office of about three-square meters. As for Larry, I didn't know where he was taken to. The officer keyed the door and left. I changed position and sat on a thread bare swivel chair bemoaning my fate. The walls were all decorated with His Majesty Yabi's pictures taken at the prime of his life. Fabrics and gadgets of the party flames lay on a cardboard at one corner. My head had begun pounding. I placed my curbed hands on the table, which had just an empty file. I then buried my head in my arms. The tears began dousing them and the table.

After about an hour, the door flung opened, and two policemen walked in. I was asked a series of questions concerning my stay in the U.S. and what I had gone there to do. All what I told them was mere blabbing. The pictures and messages in my computer and phone were used as exhibit "A" against me. I was given all kinds of names and my attempts to refute the accusations were ignored. One of the Policemen announced my charges as "disrespect for his Majesty and State Institutions, terrorism, and attempting to change the form of the State".

After the interview this first night, I was made to understand that if I did not cooperate, I would rot in jail. I stood on my initial premise—I had gone to the U.S. for an academic exchange program. Period. "Your arrogance will not set you free," they said as if rehearsed. One of them rang a bell and two young police officers came in. They were instructed to take care of me.

With the fillip of a finger, one asked me to follow them. We descended the staircase leaving behind my hand luggage. When we reached one dark corridor, they suddenly stopped in front of a door and opened it with three different keys. One pushed the door open and a pungent smell from the room propelled us to take a few steps behind. I felt like throwing up as I pinched the tip of my nose and bent down to recuperate. I was held by the shoulder and pushed inside.

When they keyed the door behind me, I collapsed on the bare floor and wept bitterly. The other occupants of the room first observed me in silence for a couple of minutes. Then some started coming to me one after the other. I heard a voice said, "Please, be strong and accept the situation for the world is not fair." I crawled to the wall and helped myself to my feet. Those who had crowded around offered some comforting words that bordered on platitudes. I thanked them for their concern.

I felt some relief when I noticed that the cell was made up of only female inmates unlike what I had heard before that men and women were bundled together in one cell. The room was however baking like an oven and smelled like a summer trash can. Though the room was well lit, the number of occupants made it darker below. Just when my eyes were getting used to the environment mosquitoes began welcoming me as if they'd been told that fresh blood was around. Since I was putting on a t-shirt, the buzzing parasites had their fair share of feasting on me.

I bowed my head, wept, and only stopped after about an hour. I had no phone, just nothing to contact the outside world. Thoughts of that increased my grief. I stopped weeping and began pondering on my fate. How long was I to be in this pit toilet? Would I ever come out? What have they charged me with? If the worst happened, how would my relations know? Have those who have come to welcome me gone back? How were they feeling? What were they thinking?

I reflected on my life in the U.S. someone had advised me not to come back because the U.S.A was heaven on earth. However, the thought of my family and new job could not let me stay. Even the nine months were ones punctuated with nostalgia and occasional regrets. I was told I could stay in the U.S. and wait for the job offer with UNESCO or claimed the situation back home was dire. In that case, I could file for my family to meet me. But according to me that would take eons of years. My mind went to the transit time in France. The place was beautiful. Africa was still thousands of years behind.

I cowered and sprawled down and closed my eyes. One could not cheat nature. In spite of the pressure and disillusionment, I began nodding and took a catnap. In my sleep, I dreamt and saw myself hugging Junior. Then I was in my husband's arms in bed. My husband was smiling at me and holding a bouquet of flowers made up of beautiful red, yellow, and pink roses. I was bombarding him with passionate kisses, and he was making some guttural noises under intense pleasure. Just when we had taken off our clothes to begin ravishing the gourmet, a man broke into our house and shot him on the head. I started screaming just to wake up to find myself on the fusty floor.

Two of the inmates were on hand to find out about my worry and comfort me. I told them where I had come from and how innocent I was. They laughed sarcastically and derided me that if I knew the condition of others in that cell I would not be whining and whimpering like a baby.

Beads of sweat formed on my forehead. "I just came from the U.S., and I have been arrested on charges ranging from spite on his Majesty and terrorism."

"Most of us here have been accused of the same reasons," one of the ladies said.

"I just want to get out of this stinking hole. No human being can survive here."

"Any crayfish survives in the pot," the same lady who had spoken said.

I stood and started jumping screaming like a mad person. The two ladies tried to hold me, but I overpowered them. I screamed so loud that two police officers took me out. They hit my head and kicked me before pulling my ears as if I were a kid.

"Why are you shouting as if you are being raped?"

"I am suffocating to death, and I miss my family."

"Ambazozo, you will die here, you dog."

"What have I done to deserve this?"

"You have done nothing," they taunted.

"Then let me go."

"Go," he mocked.

I was asked to stand but I did not budge. They manhandled and dragged me to a cubicle and asked if it was better. I pouted my lips and sighed. They looked at each other, cursed me and banged the door, keyed it and left.

CHAPTER SEVEN

A charge of adrenaline shot through me when the door to that dank room was banged against me. At first, I thought I was in a different world because I felt myself floating like an object would do in the moon. The cubicle was well lit, and I had to close my eyes for a while so that my pupils could become used to the intensity of the blinding light. When I opened my eyes, they hurt, and I had to close them again, this time tightly while groping by the wall to lean. When I could not control the tremors that had all of a sudden taken hold of me, I slumped on the floor like a heap of plantains. A weight I could not fathom settled on my heart. "God save my soul," I muttered.

When my eyes were used to the light, I tried to take stock of the downturn of events, but my mind was so distracted. The only thing on my mind was freedom. I surveyed the environment for a possible route of escape. As my eyes roved around the rectangular cage I was hemmed in, I saw two holes the size of an exercise book, which served as windows. The two openings were so close to the concrete ceiling. I was portly and not agile enough to climb the smooth grey wall. Even if I did, I could not still pass through any of those outlets. Granted that I squeezed myself, how was I to get down and walk to the tall walls that encased the police cell? Then I had to climb the palisade fortified with live barbed wires. Since my thought of escape was an adventure in futility, I hurriedly knocked it off my mind.

I thought about Larry and was just wondering what he was doing. I also imagined whether his own cell was dead silent as mine. I wondered if he was in the same cubicle like me. I decided to walk around the cubicle. It at least had a toilet. The murky floor, the clammy walls, and the mildew-infested toilet seat gave me the impression that it had not been used for a while. I was glad that I would not easily pick up a urinary infection.

Since the enclosure was just about three meters by two, I sat back on the floor wondering where the rains began to beat the Anglophones that they were made second-class citizens in their own country. La République had done everything possible to shield Southern Cameroonians from their history. It was in the Foumban Conference of 1961 that La République finally nailed the lid on the Anglophone coffin. Though I was not born then, history had it that the Southern Cameroonian delegates who attended the conference were hoodwinked into signing deals and pacts with La République without properly studying the content of the documents. Thus, they came back from the plebiscite empty-handed, as if they had gone there for a joy event. Though it was agreed at the conference that the two nations were to come together to form a Federal République of equal status, La République flouted the terms just a couple of days after the botched assembly with the hope of assimilating their English-speaking counterparts.

Since then, Anglophones had been made the scapegoat and always treated like pariahs. The head of state had come from La République since the inception of the fake union. Strategic posts like the ministers of finance, defense, national security, and territorial administration had been the sole preserve of La République. Each time Southern Cameroonians attempted to raise their heads in protest about the failed union and their marginalization, they were tortured, maimed, incarcerated, and at times decapitated just to gag them.

Though 70 percent of the country's wealth came from Southern Cameroons, they were made to feed on the crumbs of the wealth. The top positions in the oil refinery, corporations, and the administration in Southern Cameroons were manned by people from La République. Out of about 40 ministers, only four were from Southern Cameroons. Anglophones could boast only of two military generals even though the country had twenty-three generals. Almost all directors were Francophones, and a few sub-directors were Anglophones.

Tears coursed down my cheeks as I thought of all the maltreatment meted on Anglophones after joining their so-called brothers. I have a Ph.D. in History but in the eyes of La République I was still an Ordinary Level holder. No Anglophone was ever good for anything in La République. "I am sick and tired," I huffed. The words did not come out clearly because I was famished and out of breath. I was also thirsty. I looked around if there was a tap but there was none. I tried to flush the toilet to see if it was even working but it wasn't.

The journey and the malaise I were subjected to were beginning to take their toll on me. I thought of the whereabouts of my family but only felt more frustrated. I imagined how my family, in their hopelessness, had gone home not knowing what had actually happened to me. Perhaps I had remained in France. I could imagine the confusion and the argument that might have erupted between my family and the others who had come to welcome me. I supposed my husband was speechless, as he had nothing to say. I could see him in my mind's eye tossing, turning, and cursing on the sofa in the living room with Junior nestled by his chest.

With tightness in my eyes, I screamed, "What have I done?"

I could hear it echo in the dark and cold night. But no one answered. Gall began to rise in my chest.

I curbed my hands around my mouth and yelled, "I want to see my family."

When I got no response, I jumped to my feet and made to the door like a furious lioness. I banged on the metal door and waited for a response, but no one made any sound. I banged on the door several times while screaming. The same two police officers came for me.

"I want to see my family," I said emphatically.

One of the police officers wanted to hold my hand. I dodged and said, "Don't touch me."

"What is the problem?" the other police officer asked.

"Why am I here?"

"You should ask the question to the commissioner in the morning."

I felt overheated. "I want to see my son."

"Madam you're under custody," the other police officer who had been silent said.

"I am thirsty," I said.

He pointed to a bucket on a stool and told me to get water from it. When I had drunk to my fill, I went back to my moods.

"I can't stay in that stinking lonely cell," I said, dragging my hands through my hair repeatedly.

Immediately I said so, the two officers pounced on me and grabbed my wrist. I struggled to free myself, but their strength overpowered mine. I kicked this way and that, but they will not let go. Since I was screaming, another police officer came out. When he appeared, the others let go their hands off me.

"What is going on, madam?" he asked calmly.

"I want to see my family."

"Ha, so when you were rallying people to disintegrate the state you didn't think of your family?"

"I've done no such thing."

"But information gotten from your phone and laptop betray your lies."

"Having pictures as a patriotic citizen about what is going on in my country does not make me a rebel."

"You should say that in court, madam."

When the man talked about the court, my heart jumped into my hands. I took in a deep breath and waited for some time before I exhaled. "Don't die as a coward," a voice whispered to me. I jerked causing the chair to scuff the floor loudly.

"Since I know I did not commit any crime, can you take me to my home?"

"Madam you can be handcuffed for insubordination."

"I have not eaten… I have not taken a shower…those are my basic rights which you have infringed upon."

"Don't implicate yourself the more."

I flexed my fingers repeatedly. "Nobody is above the law, and nobody is a second-class citizen here."

"Shut up, you rebel leader."

"I am not a rebel and I have the right to speak."

"I wanted to make you sit in that corridor rather than the cell, but I might change my mind."

"God alone knows what you people are doing to innocent civilians."

"Go and sit over there," he waved his hand.

"I am hungry."

"Get her some bread," the man told his subordinates.

I sat at the corridor on a cushion and one of the police officers brought me some bread with a cup of sardine and a bottle of orange soda. The man assigned his subordinates to other duties, and when I had finished ravishing the bread, he called me to his office and asked me to close the door behind me. Though I was scared, I knew he could not stoop that low as to rape me since the other officers were just a stone throw. The first thing that caught my interest as I sat down was his name boldly carved in silver letters on a wooden block. Pierre Mbarga was rocking on his swivel chair as he spoke. He told me that if I cooperated, he would help me. I insisted to him that I was innocent and that I was a mere victim of circumstances.

"Madam, since your case is at this level, we can kill it here before it gets to—"

"Emmm what?" I cut in.

He took off his jutting cap and placed it on the neatly arranged table before him. He then squinted his eyes and said, "This is a serious crime against the state if you don't know."

"I am innocent."

He tapped his ball head as if he had recollected something, lowered his voice, and piped, "I don't want a beautiful girl like you to go to jail."

I surveyed my surroundings, laughed drily, and said, "Why should we be talking about jail when I am not a criminal."

"If you become my girlfriend, I can work it out."

I was upset and taken aback. "You know I am married."

He tapped his foot. "We are not talking about marriage here," he said.

"Besides, I have committed no crime."

"Do you have at least 2.5million to bail yourself out?"

I fiddled with my earring. "Did I take part in the crucifixion?"

He laughed and called my name and said, "That is if you're lucky."

"I won't go into any extramarital affair just because I want to be free from a crime I did not commit."

Mbarga licked his lips and leaned forward. "America has made you more luscious."

I looked at my body and said blankly, "Thank you."

"Just think about what I have said before it's too late."

I cleared my throat. Just when he was about to say something, the analogue phone on his table rang. He picked up the phone and from the way he held it referentially, I knew he must have been called by someone in authority.

The man had placed me in a quandary. He had asked me to either sleep with him or put down 2.5million francs CFA to be free. I began contemplating caving in his beddable demands.

I could hear his conversation. The call was directly from the presidency. The caller instructed him to keep special watch of the two cases arrested who came from America and Britain, respectively. When he hung up, he held his hand to his forehead for a minute before he could utter a word. Many things were already going through my mind. Why would the presidency be so involved in our case? I wished I could operate a gun I would have blown his skull and a thousand others and die as a hero.

He took in a deep breath and told me that my case was a bit complicated, but that he would see what he could do. I was glad I had eaves-dropped his conversation. I might have wasted a huge sum of money or soil my body for nothing, and my conscience would have haunted me forever. When I left his office, my body lumbered to the corridor as if I was plodding to the grave during my father's burial.

CHAPTER EIGHT

It was at about 4:30 am that I felt sleepy. Unfortunately, this was short-lived. By 5 am, movements from the officers coupled with noises from automobiles woke me up. Bolts of sharp pains shot through my forehead as if someone were pounding it with a pestle. I was dazed as I lay down staring at one direction but seeing nothing.

I tried to recollect the conversation I had with the Police officer. The thought of court and jail scared me to death. I have been to prison to visit some people and I had an inkling of what it felt like to be a prisoner in La République dungeons. I remembered how I'd lost appetite the first day I went to the rat hole. Most of the prisoners I saw were a bag of bones in human form. I was so frightened by the thoughts of jail that I wished for disaster to sweep across the city to kill us all.

I meditated on Mbarga's demands but the thoughts of my morals from Christian upbringing made me flinch in disbelief. AIDS and other sexually transmitted diseases further scared the hell out of me. He might have just been a scammer, a cheap opportunist astute to get the better of me. There was also no way for my family to raise 2.5 million Francs CFA to oil the lips of the forces of law and order. I was in a quandary and found myself contemplating whether to run to the lion's den or plunge into a crocodile-infested lake. The message from the presidency was frightening.

I was so engrossed in wandering thoughts that I unconsciously shouted, "I am not guilty of any wrongdoing." The noise brought in officer Mbarga. He greeted as he walked in, "*Bonjour, ma soeur. Tu as bien dormi?*" I did not respond. He greeted again and asked if I had slept well. I shook my head and immediately told him that I needed to take a shower. He said OKAY and left. Shortly after, a female officer came and asked me to follow her. She took me to a bathroom where the water therapy had an immediate effect on me. After, I was ushered back to my cubicle.

When she left officer Mbarga came to me and asked me if I needed anything. I told him that I wanted to inform my family of my where abouts. He said he could help me do that. He gave me a piece of paper to write my husband's number and give him. He took the paper away only to come back a couple of minutes to tell me that the phone was ringing but my husband was not picking up the call. I was more worried. It was typical of my husband not to pick up calls from strange numbers. However, I thought that at that instant he would have been ready to clutch on a reptile.

Mr. Mbarga told me to wait for about ten minutes to try myself. After ten minutes, he sent for me. When I came, he gave me his phone and asked me to sit down. I looked at the sofa, the mahogany table full of books, and a gun leaning on the wall and was frightened to sit. I tried calling my husband's number, but it did not go through. When Mr. Mbarga tried to argue that the same number had been going through moments ago before I came in, I tried to verify but realized that he had copied the number wrongly. Every part of my body right down to my hair began brewing as he told me to go and wait in my lonely cell. I folded my hands around my chest and focused on the white-tiled clean floor.

"Madam leave."

I did not budge.

"I will see what to do." He opened some files. "Let me complete this report."

He rang the bell, and a junior officer escorted me to my cell.

The duty officers for the day started trickling in as I could hear them exchanging greetings. Mbarga finished with his report and brought one of the officers to my cell to show me to him. This new officer was a tall, dark man whose dark complexion and marks on his face revealed exactly where he came from— Far North. I immediately looked up to his nametag, which read Officer Mohamed Abdulai. He did not utter a word to me but kept snorting like a wounded rhinoceros. The way his eyes darted across his forehead sent me to the restroom. When I came back, he still stood the same way I had left him. I whispered, "Almighty God intervene." Mr Mbarga told him that I appear calm, but that instructions had come from the presidency to place double sets of eyes on me. Then Mbarga and the officer left closing the door behind them.

I was at my doldrums after they left. I still could not fathom why the presidency should be so particular about me. I was in contemplation until about an hour when my door creaked opened, and the Goliath of an officer instructed me to follow him. As I stood to go, I realized my legs were heavy. He shouted slurs at me, and I had to drag the legs as I trailed behind him.

He took me to a room that had nothing except a table and some chairs where four investigators were already waiting for me. My heart started pounding and I could hear it myself in spite of the noise around. He asked me to sit on a chair facing the officers. They had pens and files ready to take down whatever statement or the least guttural sound I made. When the officer who brought me left, there was some silence for about three minutes and then suddenly one of the officers asked me if I was

Yenyuy Mathilda? When I opened my mouth, words did not come out. I nodded and he verified the document in front of him, held the pen around his mouth and shook his head.

The first officer said, "We expect truthful answers from you, do you understand?"

"Yes."

"What did you go to do in America?" He asked rubbing his hands and looking at me intently.

"For an academic exchange program" I said.

He took a deep breath and asked, "Which places did you go to?"

I fidgeted with my blouse, bit my lips and said nothing.

"Speak, dumb," two of the interrogators shouted at once.

My chief interrogator motioned them to stay calm. He then piqued at me, and I responded, "Visiting friends."

He doodled with his pen, peered at me, and said, "*A bon!*"

I creased my face and said nothing.

He then swung around backing me with his hands to his chest and said, "Then?"

"Nothing happened," I said angrily.

"Be careful the way you talk," he huffed.

"Yes sir."

He faced me and asked, "Which political meetings did you attend?"

I stood like a statue. He then asked the second time, and I still did not respond. His colleagues were jittery. He sipped some water and placed the cup on the table with a thud. I was nervous and started blinking several times. The room was noise proof, as one could not hear any sound from outside and the thick ceiling loomed precariously as if it would swallow us. He waited for half a minute and when I was not responding he banged at the table spilling the water, which soiled some files. That was when I knew that a legless grasshopper could not be free from the beaks and talons of ravenous birds because the beast took a better of the two other officers. They immediately pounced on me, one grabbing my hair and the other yanking my hand. They pummeled my head on the wall while kicking me and shouting sneeringly, "Ambazoozoo, Ambazoozoo". I screamed, yelled, kicked, and agitated to no avail. Just when I thought that they were about stopping the torture, the main interlocutor slapped me, and the world disappeared before my eyes. Somewhere in another planet, I could hear them teasing and mocking *"Anglofool want divide country. Get up, terrorist."* This barking was followed by a kick on my waist.

The main interlocutor asked his two colleagues if they think that I am dangerous, and they confirmed by saying that women are the deadliest of the Ambazonia fighters and revolutionaries. One of them then said that they would do everything for me to cough out the ringleaders abroad, and the plans I went to hatch in America. My heart jumped to the floor, and I knew it was the end though I lay still on the floor. After a few minutes, one-stepped on my finger and I jerked as if I had been electrocuted. He lifted me up like a pumpkin and slumped me on the seat; my bum almost gave way. The chief interlocutor paced in the stuffy office for a while before landing on his swivel chair. He furrowed his face, looked at me intently and said, "Madam this issue concerns the state…I wish you knew how grievous it is."

Amidst sniffles and hiccups, I stammered, "I swear, I am inno-"

"Shallup, chien," one of the officers insulted and poked his finger on my jaw.

The main interlocutor leaned forward, adjusted his walkie-talkie hanging across his shoulders and snarled, "Who are you hobnobbing with?"

I bit my nail.

"You're a gang leader!" the hotheaded colleague of the main interlocutor barked.

I shrugged my shoulders in confusion.

"Nobody plays with Onana here and goes unscathed," the main interlocutor said, beating his chest.

I cleared my throat.

Onana the main interlocutor asked, "Who are the ring leaders you met and how much did they give you?"

I shifted my position on the chair while looking at my knee. When I raised my head, I saw the other officer addressing Onana referentially while looking at the floor. Onana was nodding as they spoke. Afterwards, he told them to teach me a lesson if that was what I wanted. All the blood in me dried up. "Get her out of my sight," he screamed. I was scared and moved backwards tumbling.

One of the officers became furious and warned that if I did not speak the truth, the four of them would make me talk through my nose and rectum. I did not know what he meant by making me talk through those places. After this warning, the interrogator continued with his questions.

"Who are your leaders?"

"To the best of my knowledge, I don't know anybody who is the leader of any group."

He did not seem satisfied with my responses and ordered two of his junior officers to make "This Anglophone talk." The two officers brought a bucket of icy water and dipped my face in it. When I was gasping for breath, they pulled my head out and jolted me. One hit my head thrice with a truncheon before asking me to stand, but I remained glued to the floor. He tugged my hair and plastered me to the wall while shouting, "Talk now or I kill you."

"I am ino . . . inno . . . innocent."

He held my apical vein and was about snuffing life out of me when I threw up before he let go. I started crying. He asked me to use my buttocks to clean the mess. I hesitated. He said it was the second time and kicked my feet. This brought me down to my knees like a bag of sawdust.

He took the truncheon from his colleague and charged towards me, but his colleagues restrained him. I had already made my last prayer because I would not have survived the blow.

"What does this imbecile think she is?" He barked while straightening his jacket.

"Can you speak before it's too late?" His colleague corroborated.

"I've done nothing wrong," I squealed.

The officer who would torture me the most emitted a wan smile, laughed drily and placed one of his boots on the chair.

He looked at his colleagues and said, "Let's eliminate this thing before she continues to pollute the others."

I recoiled when I heard this. "God wherever you are, descend now," my lips twitched.

"It's even easy because no one knows her whereabouts," another said.

The officer reiterated to me to say the truth. I repeated that I did not know any leaders, and nobody was sponsoring me. This angered him the more, and he slapped my jaw and blood began oozing out of my nostrils. I started wailing and the officers banged the door behind them promising to come for my head.

I continued weeping for about thirty minutes until they came back. My main interlocutor's eyes looked devilish this time more than they were when he started questioning me. He was overweight and looked like Idi Amin, the late dictator of Uganda. I tried to stop crying but intermittent sniffles betrayed my efforts. He warned that he would whip my soles with a blunt machete if I did not admit my guilt and lay bare whatever information I was hiding in my guts. I had come to my tether's end and was ready to pay the ultimate prize. I made up my mind not to respond to any question.

After asking a few questions with no response, he told his subordinates to "Show this Anglofoo something." The two police Officers asked me to follow them, but I remained glued to the floor. They pulled me back to my cell kicking and slapping my back all the time. When we got to the cell, they closed the door and treated me as a punching bag. They kicked, slapped, and punched. I wept until I was only sniffing. They began fondling my breasts and other erogenous zones. They said they would spare me some time to change my mind and speak the truth. Before they left, I lay sprawled on the floor like mashed potatoes.

Later that evening I was hooded, handcuffed, and bundled into a car to an unknown destination. When my face was uncovered after arriving the place my heart jumped to my palms as I could barely see *Prison Centrale* inscribed on the wall in the office where those officers kept me.

CHAPTER NINE

Nothing significant happened in the office at *Prison Centrale*, but for the fact that I was treated like a circus animal. Even though I arrived there at night within minutes, influx of soldiers, police officers, and prison administrators flooded the office in turns to look at the *"femme terroriste,"* as I would all of a sudden be referred to. My face reddened each time I heard those taunting remarks.

I just could not withstand the gazing eyes. A sheen of sweat settled on my forehead. Most of the officers peeped by the window or door, threw this or that insult or slang, clasped their hands in bewilderment and left. A few spat on my hair saying I would rot in jail. Within minutes, my hair had curled from spittle and phlegm.

When the tension and cacophony died down, male and female wardens strutted in and told me that I was to be taken somewhere to pass the night pending registration the following day. So, saying, they asked me to follow them. I took in a cleansing breath as I trod behind.

When we got to one door after passing through many convoluted corridors, the lady took off my handcuffs and the man opened the door and asked me to get in. I hesitated. He looked at his watch as if to say time was of the essence.

"Get in fast," the lady snarled to my utter shock.

"Ha when you were busy rallying people against his Majesty the Supreme Head of state and to divide the country, you didn't know the consequences, *femme terroriste!*" the man said.

I was too tired and numbed by the torture and sheer shock to even respond.

"Get in fast," she shoved me and screamed.

I cringed my mouth in annoyance, glowered at her insolence but did not budge. She folded the hands of her thick long sleeve khaki jacket. The man blocked her from using force on me. I plodded to the well-lighted room that looked more like a trench. When he banged the door behind him and keyed it, I could hear the overzealous lady shouting at the top of her voice that she would have taught me a lesson if I had continued to be stubborn.

Since my legs could barely support my frame, I buried my buttocks on the floor curling my toes to release tension. Then the pains on my wrist where the handcuffs held me firmly drew my attention to the spot. I could see welts on my wrists. I sighed deeply and clasped my knees tightly together. The area looked reddish pale. My matted hair bobbed as I tried to shake off my frustration. I closed my eyes tightly and tried to forget everything happening to me. Though it seemed an adventure in futility, several attempts bore some fruits. I had to practice this technique several times before I could catch some sleep. I do not know if it was the yoga that gave me some respite or a combination of it and extreme lassitude.

What woke me up from slumber was a dream. In the reverie, I was placed in a dungeon that could only fit my size. The cell had spikes on the walls and ceiling. Each movement I made landed the prickly objects in my flesh. Worse, the guards had poured some itchy liquid on my bare body. The only way to ease the irritation was to rub my body on the spikes, but since I was in chains it made movement difficult. The door to the cell was not bolted. The only way of escape was to turn around and open the door. I did while tearing my flesh. Immediately I stepped out, someone raised an alarm and a soldier fired at me. That was when I woke up doused in sweat.

I could not make out the meaning of the nightmare. I sat on the bare clammy floor too dazed. I could hear footsteps and noises all over the building. I guessed it was dawn. As minutes glided, I wondered what would become of me. I had become a prisoner without a crime. Suddenly, I heard some footsteps stomping towards my cell. My blood pressure rose to a crescendo.

The steps halted at the door to the cell I was languishing in. I heard the locks on the door creaking. When the door was pulled open, the female warden piqued at me, pouted her lips and sighed. She then handcuffed me and said I should follow her to the registration office. As we stepped out, she said, "Respect yourself because if you play dirty, I will play dirty."

I cleared my throat sarcastically.

Behold, at the registration office, I met Larry and a couple of people. He smiled when he saw me. I wondered what amused him because both his legs and hands were handcuffed. Welts spotted his face, and his jaw was swollen. His sight reminded me of Patrice Lumumba the Congo-Kinshasa Nationalist who was killed by his fellow compatriots with the connivance of the U.S and Belgian government.

"This is La République," he said using his lips to point at the chains around him.

I emitted a wan smile and said defiantly, "God will see us through for a clear conscience has no fear."

The others giggled. That was when I really noticed them- two ladies and six men. They all sat on a crescent shaped bench. The lady who brought me left and just the potential prisoners I had met were waiting in the room which looked like a hallway.

The ladies were in their thirties. Two of the men were in their sixties and other two in their twenties. They looked hungry and haggard.

"If this is the price, we shall pay to liberate our people from more than 57 years of subjugation, so be it," one of the oldest men on the bench said.

"Yes," the others chorused.

My chest loosened and I squeezed my forehead. That remark drew my attention to the fact that everyone in the room was a Southern Cameroonian and that La République was bent on eliminating us. When the others noticed that Larry and I were picked up at the airport they were so excited to hear our stories. We too were excited to hear theirs. Tata Banla said they arrested him in Jakiri, Mekolle said he was whisked off in Kumba, Atem said he was arraigned in Allo, aged Pa Agbor said he was taken from his farm in Muyuka, Nawain Buh said they decapitated her husband before whisking her off from Kom, while Bih said she was picked up in Bafut.

I could imagine the gory tales these detainees were harboring. I guessed such firsthand experiences could form an interesting book for progeny. I was already itchy to hear their versions of arrests, torture, and eventual transfer to Yaoundé. But for the meantime I wanted to know what happened to Larry the last time we separated. Just when I turned to him to ask what happened and how it had been with him, a warden and a police officer appeared. The warden told us to be patient and that they would soon get back to us since they were deliberating on the different cells we would be sent to. I bowed my head and muffled, "So, my doom is sealed?"

When they turned their backs, I asked Larry to tell me about his baptism of fire. He yawned even though looking confident. I could see the other companions adjusting themselves and looking at each other to hear a *bush faller* just landing from the airplane talk about his brutal encounter with La République army.

Larry emitted a wry smile exposing his conspicuous dimples planted on his chubby jaws. My thoughts flashed on Junior because he inherited his parent's dimples. Larry then adjusted himself and the chain on his feet and hands clanged. I looked away as my eyes pooled. I fought back the tears fiercely.

"How I survived that night is a miracle," were Larry's first words.

I thought of my agony too that night and Mr. Mbarga's half-baked favor. I could imagine poor Larry's troubles if I passed the night at the corridor and still complained. He then curved his back like an armadillo for us to look. I flinched when Mekolle lifted Larry's T-shirt and exposed the ridges on his back. It appeared there were marks from an iron rod.

"What happened?" I screamed.

"As soon as they bolted the door behind you, one of the guards kicked my shin bone. I wanted to fight back but the guards restrained and rough handled me. That was very brief though. What you see on my back is not caused by guards or wardens."

The expression on our faces changed.

"What happened?" Pa Agbor asked. The others scratched their heads.

"Other inmates," was Larry's answer.

We all looked at each other. I formed my lips twice to ask a question, but the words stuck in my throat. The others too were too dazed and nonplussed to say anything.

"I was shoved into a cell within a cell that had two ferocious inmates. The iron cell was like a cage and its black walls were made of iron. When I stepped in, the two guys with matted hair did not even wait for the door to close before they could begin torturing me. I guess they were hardened criminals who had nothing to lose because I became their punching bag even when we had not exchanged words. They dragged me and started torturing and molesting me. I fought back. One pinned my neck between his legs while the other used his elbow to dig the trenches you see on my back." He lifted his shirt and showed us the swollen portions. I was broken. He continued his gory tale.

"Then they pressed my back on the iron wall. At one time, I almost gave up, but a smart idea came to my mind, and I managed to clutch one of the inmate's navel, which was as monstrous as the scrotum of a pig. He screamed, but I clung to it as a giant rabid insect would hang on a prey. He kicked and cried, but I did not give up. The other inmate rained blows on my back, but I did not budge. Like a typical Ambazonia, I stood my ground, squeezing his navel tighter. Then the other inmates started banging on the wall like maddened beasts. Four heavily armed guards rushed to the scene."

"How long did this last?"

Larry held his face as if he'd smell the excrement of a duck and said, "Not up to three minutes, but I was prepared to go down with those animals."

"Hm, thank God for you," I said as I clasped my hands and bit my lips.

"Since I did not die that night, I don't think I will ever die," Larry quipped.

"But why would they send you to be with demons?" Pa Agbor asked.

Larry looked around vapidly. "Ha, I believe it was my own baptism of fire."

"They wanted to kill you," I said.

"God said nay because this struggle has been ordained by the Almighty," Bih said.

"What happened after?" Tata Banla asked.

Larry flinched, perhaps from the pains caused by the chain; he managed to wipe his lips and said, "I was in another beehive, but the purgatory type."

"How?" Bih who appeared to be lost cut in.

Just when Larry was about to begin his tale of woes, two wardens walked in officiously and commanded us to line up. We obeyed like nursery school pupils.

CHAPTER TEN

When we got to the registration center, the prison officials separated the men from the women. Our group made up of Bih, Nawain, and me was guided to a large, dilapidated room with flaking walls and broken windowpanes. The female wardens told us to sit and wait for our names to be called up. As I scoured for a clean spot to rest my bum on the metal chair, my eyes fell on the squalid floor, and I grunted in disgust. The plump Nawain, looked like she was in her early thirties, appeared relaxed though she was clearing her throat continuously. Bih was dark and thin, and from every indication, she had been going through the Stations of the Cross all her life. Not only her hair was poorly plaited, but her blouse was also torn, and her weather-beaten skirt horribly twisted. She was shaking every part of her fragile frame like a reed being tossed by a fast-moving stream. Though poverty and suffering had crushed her to the scum of the earth, I could discern that natural beauty in her that polishing and make-up could transform into a paragon of beauty. She was polished black – the kind of blackness that if properly nourished could send men tumbling in gutters or sidewalks.

As for me, I was in a different planet. It appeared as if only my shadow rested its tingling buttocks on the bench aligned with iron rods. I tried to initiate a discussion but realized that none of us had the wherewithal to speak. Just when I decided to relax over working my already charged brain, a scrawny man, the age of my grandfather, toddled out of one room and pronounced my name in a strange accent. First, I was too dazed by the man's age and gait, and secondly by his uniform which hung on his frail body like a scarecrow, making him a living caricature. When the stooping gnarled and osseous fellow piped again in his shrill voice like that of someone whose vocal cords have been ripped off, I stood up. He piqued at me through his over-sized antique goggles and sighed. He beckoned to me as one would a pet. My guts churned.

As I lumbered towards him shaking my head vigorously, I knew that my doom was sealed. All along, I had been in denial. It was a different Yenyuy who trudged to the tiny room facing a man and a woman and a police officer. The woman appeared to be a nurse because she was donned in white and a crown on her head. She took my weight, height, blood pressure, pulse. I knew it was just for formality because the equipment was not only archaic but also not functioning properly as she kept pressing the power button many times for it to come on.

Her companion was busy casting lecherous glances at me and licking his lips furtively as he ogled. A lump formed in my throat, and I swore within me that if he dared me I would take him to the cleaners. After registering some information about my birth, family, and hometown, she handed me to her colleague; the lustful male who questioned me further. After that, the lady handed a plastic bag to me with prison garments inside. She pointed to a cubicle adjacent and told me to go in and measure them. To me that was the final lowering of the coffin to mother earth. I just could not understand how La République had already judged and condemned me as a terrorist without any investigation or alibi. I reluctantly put on the red jacket and the red pants and came out to show her and her colleagues. They nodded and asked me to sign some papers.

It was then that I mustered courage and asked them if I had been sentenced without a crime and without a hearing. They said I was under detention pending investigation, which would amount to trips in military courts in downtown Yaoundé. From there the judge, with directions from the supreme head of state, would determine how many years we would spend behind bars, if we were lucky not to be hanged. The warden reminded me of the terrorism law in La République which stated unequivocally that anybody caught perpetuating state terrorism or sponsoring it or even associating with anyone connected to the "vile practice" would face the firing squad.

"Kill me now," I heard something echoed in my ears before I realized that I'd actually said that.

"Kill who and why?" the nurse asked.

"When you were raising funds abroad and insulting the head of state you didn't know you will die?" the officer asked.

"Kill yourself," the nurse taunted to my utter consternation.

"Kill me, blood sucking maniacs," I screamed.

"You've not yet seen anything," the other man who had been quiet and leering at me said.

I creased my face and clasped my hand on the table. "What a lawless state," I said. By this time, I was no longer afraid of anything. "You think you are omnipotent to just treat humans as parasites?" I shouted and began a tirade of how I went to the U.S for academic reasons and came back only to be held and detained by a bunch of lunatics and wastrels for something I had no idea of. They were not even willing to listen because after my babbling which was more of a monologue, they said they were merely doing what they had been assigned to do and that I could sing my choir, "*faux chorale*" as they called it, in the military court when time would come.

I wished I was with my talons, then one of them, especially the lady would have gone down to Hades that same moment before I followed. I bit my finger in my imagination and sighed repeatedly.

The lady told me that those uniforms were my prison clothes and that I should wear them within the confines of the prison and each time we had an official outing. She then told me to go and wait in the lobby, which reminded me of "Winter Nightfall" by J. C. Squire. The pain on the clammy wall was flaked and the ruptured ceiling leaked. The ceiling also had brown marks from the leakages. The lady said soon we would be allocated our various cells. I took in a deep breath, made the sign of the cross and cursed the day Southern Cameroon joined La République.

As I stepped out in my new outfit, Nawain, in a freaky appearance, burst into tears and immediately lay sprawled on the dusty floor. At first, I thought she had heard some bad news. She began squalling and rolling like a drum when I came closer. The officials who just attended to me pushed past me and held her. Unfortunately for them Nawain was a squaw and had the strength of a lion. Her one move sent the people scampering for safety. She was agitating and saying they abducted her husband, sliced his throat on camera, and took her away alleging that she was housing terrorists.

When the police officers tried in vain to subdue her, they shamefully called for backup. Before the three hefty and heavily armed men could come, the devil had taken the better of Nawain and she had plunged on the scrotum of one of the police officers who clucked his gun due to searing pains.

He wailed, kicked, squirmed, and begged but Nawain's grip was that of a tick. It was only when one of the soldiers grabbed her throat that she let go. By that time the officer was already astride the bridge to the underworld. His pupils had disappeared, and he was gasping for breath and twitching. Nawain was immediately handcuffed and taken away while the others concentrated on performing cardiovascular pulmonary resuscitation on the officer. When the officer was about regaining consciousness, they carried him away.

As my buttocks itched on the rough bench, I could only wonder the fate that might befall Nawain. She was already in jail to be jailed. I exchanged a few words with Bih who sounded quite interesting and reassuring. She briefed me of the woes she had gone through after losing the leg of a younger brother shot on the day of the so-called "CPDM Unitary March." She said her father was a retired grade one teacher who had gone to Yaoundé a million times for his pension in vain. And that she was the eldest of five children who were looking up to her. I tried to find out from her about her level of education and her means of subsistence, but she only narrated experiences that made me cry. She said she was working in a cooperative union as a cashier and when thieves broke into the place and carted away with the safe, she was dragged to court where the magistrate spoke only in French-a language she did not understand.

"Can you be more explicit and even tell me how you got here?" I asked.

Developing interest in others' problems gave me some solace just as psychologists say that misery loves company. As Bih readied herself to tell me her court palaver and how she was arrested, the same ropy fellow whose legs were astride the grave came for her. She indicated to me that there would be time for storytelling. When she got up, her symmetrical built and voluptuous hips stroke a cord in my heart. "This is beauty wasting," I said to myself. My wish was to connect her to my cousin who had graduated from the Higher Teachers Training College and was searching for a wife. However, I gave myself sometime to study her first.

As I waited for her, my mind drifted to my own *wahala*. My troubles beneath the stars were many, and a tsunami of them seemed to be on the way. I bowed my head as the lyrics of "Swing Low Sweet Chariot" kept bombarding my thumping forehead. I tried to mutter a prayer, but my tongue was stuck on the roof of my mouth. I began humming the song I had resisted all the while.

CHAPTER ELEVEN

As I sat in the lobby waiting for Bih, the coarse seat could not permit me be at ease. I kept changing posture sending my weight to one side and then the other. I used both hands to support my jaws. I felt spittle form into a gob in my otherwise dry mouth. I waddled by the window and flung the mess outside. I crawled back to my seat and buried my head between my laps whimpering. My thoughts wandered. To be an Anglophone in Cameroun was to be sidelined in all spheres and treated as the dregs of humanity – the scum of the earth. He is the last to be hired and first to be fired. Underrepresented in the government, but over expected to deliver. He cannot be head of state and cannot hold sensitive positions in the state like minister of defense, finance, and communication.

Throughout each stage of my detention and interrogation from the airport, I had been dreaming. The full weight of the severity of my fate hung over my head like a dark shadow as I stood, sat and paced up and down. My blood was seething from the crown of my hair to the soles of my numbed feet. "God when will an Anglophone have a voice in this country?" I asked as I steadied my gaze on the floor. From somewhere in the netherworld, I heard a shrill voice, "Mathilda wake up."

Then someone shook my shoulder violently.

I cleared my stone face to see Bih towering above me.

"This is the third time I am screaming your name." I waved to her not to bother me. "*Lif me yaa my sister*," I said and buried my head in between my laps, convulsing in tears.

She sat and whispered closer. "We have to be strong," she elbowed me and spoke. "One of the worst things you can do to your enemies is to make them see your tears. Let us rather sing praises like Paul and Silas in prison."

I smiled wryly. "What's up?" I said still staring at the squalid floor.

"As you can see, these are my prison clothes," Bih said as if she was joking.

I took in a deep breath as I lifted my head. The coffin had been lowered to the grave by the pallbearers, and it was now left for the grave diggers to begin pouring earth to fill the infinitely dark tomb. I tried to speak haltingly but lost my words halfway. I mumbled inconsistently before holding Bih as a support to stand. She could not support my weight, so I buckled and slumped back to the seat and remained motionless. In that brief instance, I was transmuted, and ferried to the world beyond. I saw myself moving in a dark tunnel as if being remote controlled. Bih shook me hard and I woke up like a corpse being resurrected. My stomach was tightening and hardening. "I wish I could fight back," I whispered to myself.

"So, it has come to this," I muttered.

Bih just stared at me as an HIV patient may pique at the medical practitioner who had declared his or her serology status to be positive. I could see her feet trembling and her thin lips twitching as she drowned beside me. She frayed and wiped the tip of her pointed nose. She placed her hands by her side. Put them down. A few minutes she lifted them on her head. A certain indescribable force crawled through my veins making them taut. They began building resistance in me.

"We shall overcome," I said jutting my chest out.

"Mathilda are you all right?" Bih probably taken aback asked. "What has come over you?"

"Nothing."

As I curled my lips to utter some words of defiance, a soldier, a male warden, and two female wardens approached us. From every indication, they were mere executioners to carry out the orders of their boss. I jumped to my feet, opened my arms wide and told them I was ready before they could even utter a word.

"Follow us," one of them thundered, "You bitch."

We marched behind them in silence. We walked through long and winding melancholic and cluttered corridors before stepping to an open space. Just when we were about entering another corridor, I saw something that drained my blood—a human being partly covered with rusted corrugated iron sheets. When I noticed that the carcass sprawled disrespectfully on the floor was that of Nawain I stood petrified. She has been killed almost the same way as her husband just that her neck was not severed from her body. Her eyes were gouged out. I needed to be convinced that life had been snuffed out of her like an ant's. Bih too stood, dazed like one whose soul was about to jump out of her mortal being. The guards pushed us to move and then hauled some slurs at us.

"Bitch too." I retorted and crossed my arms over my chest.

A kick on my buttocks was the response. I staggered and moved faster.

As we moved on, I noticed the buildings looked like some ancient battlements and gothic castles. The only people we met were wardens, guards and soldiers. Soldiers stood on rooftops holding guns and looking tensed. Some stood on turrets and their eyes darted like hazard lights. The patrol was tight as we edged our way to whatever fate awaited us. I tried to speak but was choked with rage. Bih supported her waist with both hands. I placed my hand on her shoulder. That was enough encouragement. But she burst into tears and leant on a pillar. I sniffed and held her hands. The female wardens shouted at us that there was no time to waste.

We passed by a ramshackle building with the words Kosovo carved conspicuously on its wall with baked excrement. I wondered whether it was a pigsty or a dumping heap for refuse. The flaking paint together with the lurid walls made the building creepier. As we approached the building, the noisome stench proved unbearable. Even the guards and the wardens had to close their nostrils with their hands. After the dilapidated structure, we traipsed for about ten meters before meeting Baghdad. It was even worse. I wondered what such a structure could be harboring if not corpses. The thing was merely hanging as if it could crash at any time though it looked fortified with pillars surrounding it. We skirted around the building, passed through some makeshift stalls and approached Guantanamo. It was secluded and surrounded by barbed wires. We stood at the entrance and waited before some guards opened the frightening gate for us to trudge in. It was here that while we were still waiting, we heard some clanging and turned to look. Behold our eyes fell on Larry, Pa Agbor, and Tata Banla in fetters. Larry's pen immediately caught my attention. I thought it was a magic biro because no one had taken it from him.

They were excited to see us as they smiled. Since smiles were noted to be contagious, we mustered courage and exuded wan smiles too. As we passed through the gate, I knew only our obituaries would be read if that last respect to our memory could even be possible. Larry's upper lip was swollen, and caked blood hung loosely on his mouth. Pa Agbor was staggering as he limped. The cap he had worn the first time I met him was no longer on his grey hair. He told the guards repeatedly to go for his glasses, but no one cared to listen. Instead, the guards shouted at him calling him names ranging from terrorist to secessionist.

"So, it has really come to this?" I said.

Larry stared at me and said, "It will be all right."

A soldier stamped his boots on the poorly plastered yard and shushed us with the following scream: "*Shallop, les anglos la lock ya mop.*"

I glowered at him and sighed.

"Move faster," a warden said.

"*Vite!*" a soldier shouted pushing us to move faster.

Slowly we approached the large veranda of the building. A corridor separated the building. We were taken to the left while Larry and the others were taken to the right. At the lobby, which looked like a stall visited by a tsunami, a man registered our names in a thick crumpled book. The two female wardens who brought us kept emphasizing that each time we had to go out we must wear the prison clothes. I let out a hard sigh and closed my eyes. Two soldiers ushered us to the gulag, opened the set of iron doors and let us in.

We could barely find a place to stand in the well-lighted hall. The smell of sweat mixed with stale food made matters worse. The place was oppressively hot. Some of the inmates sat on pieces of cardboard papers while some lay on dirt thin mattresses. We were shivering. The walls stood tall like a giant palisade guarding a medieval castle. The ceiling boards were hanging precariously like the dry branches of a dead palm. After surveying the place as if we had been transported to a different planet, one lady whose mattress was thicker than those of others beckoned on us.

Bih looked at me as I looked at her. We trudged towards her like people attending their own funeral. When we stood before her it seemed as if one was standing before Herod who would want nothing short of one's head on a platter of gold. Her sunken eyes, the way she was blinking them, her disheveled hair and her manly features frightened the hell out of us.

"New man tax," she held her open palm before us and shouted in her stentorian voice.

I looked at Bih who had concentrated on her toes.

"Don't you understand French?"

I hurriedly nodded signifying that I do.

She spoke in broken Pidgin English typical of rustics. "*You bring wati for Bamnda, Buyaa?*"

We sat nonplussed.

She switched back to French, her crossed eyes moving like Christmas lights. "Am I talking to humans or stones? I said what have you brought from *Bamnda* and *Buyaa*?"

None of us responded.

She jerked from her position, craned forward exposing a lipoma on her neck that was the size of a golf ball. Bih took some steps behind though the lady was merely changing her sitting position.

"What have you brought to the Queen of Sarajevo?"

"We were taken unawares," I said weakly throwing up my hands.

"No one comes here prepared."

She closed her eyes for half a minute. When she opened them, she felt like using the rest room. Luck fell our way. A fight erupted between two inmates over a piece of tattered loin. Each person was claiming ownership. A tug of war ensued. With the little space available in the crowded gulag, each move of the fighters sent people to the floor. Most of the inmates had run to one corner. All of a sudden, the manly woman interrogating us hollered, "Stop." The two women involved in the melee stood petrified and the loin dropped from their hands instantly.

"Bring it here."

Both women bent at once as if remote-controlled.

"On your knees," she screamed.

Like tired sheep, they all went down. She then told one lady beside us to bring the loin. When it was brought, she told the two women that none of them would ever have it. She asked them to stand. She then turned to us and said, "You mean to say you have nothing?"

"Like what?" Bih asked. I nudged her to be silent.

"I control this place," she said. "I've been here for eighteen years. To render your life a bit comfortable here, you must pay your new man tax."

I could not wrap my mind on the bit of comfort she was talking about since the place, to me, was already worse than the grave and we were at our tether's end.

"For the last time, how much do you have?"

"Our relations do not even know we are here," I said.

"Spare me that crap, you Biafra," she cursed.

I squinted at her devilish brow.

"Anglofou," she said.

"Once our relations are contacted, we will give you something," I said entreatingly.

She faced the moldy dark wall. Her buttocks hung on her back like the hunch of a heifer. Still in that posture, she said, "Until then."

Our faces brightened. "Please, don't make life difficult for us here," I pleaded.

She did not respond, though she turned around.

I stood staring at the black and tanned face filled with freckles, and a chin covered with a beard like a man's.

"Where are we going to sleep?" Bih asked.

"Syria, and specifically in Aleppo," she responded.

Bih and I looked at each other, completely lost.

"I say go to Syria," she said and swung around pointing to a corridor which was poorly lighted.

We stood planted on the spot as if a spell had been cast on us.

"Go and meet the pastor," she screamed.

We moved like a little flock of only two. The corridor was close to the toilet, which had no door. A reedy looking woman leant on the stained wall. A few shattered and lean cartoons lay on the floor of the corridor. The scrawny fellow smiled and beckoned on us to come. We lumbered towards, completely defeated.

Bih sank down like some human waste. I flopped down too. The woman who had supported her torso on the wall crept towards us. She gave us some comforting words quoting extensively from the Bible. She talked about Joseph, Shadrach, Meshach, and Abednego and ended her lecture with Daniel. She said she was not afraid of the one who only had access to the body, as God permitted, but could not touch the soul. She told us not to worry because the Egyptians we were seeing would be seen no more. "I know my redeemer liveth," she concluded.

Since she was so open and encouraging, I decided to open up to her. She allayed our worries and cited ex-ministers who thought they were the untouchables only to be languishing in that same prison they neglected to upgrade. She said whatever His Majesty Yabi and clique were doing was kicking against the pricks because God would strike them when His time would come.

"God can never be mocked," she hissed.

When I asked her about her name and how she found herself in that dungeon, she said her name was Eposi. I asked again how she was arrested; she broke into tears. Bih and I could not withstand her sniffles. We too burst into tears. After crying out our lungs, she said amidst sniffles that she would tell us some other time.

"So how long have you been here?" Bih asked

"Three weeks."

"How do you sleep?" Bih asked again.

I did not wait for her to answer. "How do you cope?"

She wiped her tears with the back of her hand. "God will sustain us."

"Amen," we chorused.

We held hands and entreated God's mercies upon our lives. When we were done, Eposi promised to tell us her story the following day. I was weak and famished.

"When will they serve us food?" I asked.

Eposi laughed sarcastically clapped her hands and said, "Food?"

"Hm, but the stench…"

"Your lungs will become used to."

I have come to my tether's end. I could not come to terms with the dichotomy of life. Not long ago I was in Uncle Sam's Country feeling on top of the world, the wealthiest and the strongest country in the world. It was all frolicking and rollicking. I had visited touristic sites in Lower Manhattan in New York and had even gone to the Empire State Building before visiting the Pentagon and President JF Kennedy's final resting place at Arlington National Cemetery. I had eaten French fries, pizza, biscuits, hot Cheetos and a lot of American stuff whose stories I had planned to share back home; lots of exciting stories that were becoming faint and even sour to me now. I buried my head in my laps as I felt my soul melting.

CHAPTER TWELVE

The next day we woke up as early as 5 am though Bih and I did not sleep at all. My back ached and my feet hurt excruciatingly because I had been standing up most of the night. I could not still believe that Nawain had just died like a chicken. The heat and the noise made by the inmates plus the noisome smell could not let a sleeping dog lie. However, I had heard other inmates snoring despite the inconvenience. This made me believe Albert Camus's words that a face that toils so close to stone is itself stone.

Eposi told us that with only two bathrooms for more than fifty inmates, the earlier one did one's toiletries the better because the fighting in the shower was horrible. She said one inmate was dragged out of the bathroom naked and beaten until she bled because she wasted a lot of time in the shower. She told us that by 6:30am, we had to be at the chapel for private or group morning devotion and at 7:30am, we would go for breakfast. After that, we would go back to the Chapel for general devotion.

"The door closes at 8am and that's that," she said.

"Are we in a military camp?"

Eposi crossed her arms across her chest. "This is more than a military camp."

I closed my eyes and lifted my hands above my head, "The God of heaven, are you alive and seeing what your children are going through?"

She took her shower at a Panasonic speed. Bih took hers in the same speed. When I went for mine, I thought I was fast too until one inmate ripped the door open and dragged me out, my body doused in soap foams. I wanted to fight back but Eposi winked that I should ignore. "Only a lunatic would follow a mad man, naked, to the marketplace because he'd run with his clothes," she had later told me.

When everyone was almost ready, the squaw who molested us, the night before screamed, "Wear your name tags on your chests." Those who had not done obeyed the military command instantaneously. We stuck ours to the chests of our uniforms.

"Ha, prisoner of conscience," Eposi said to me.

"Prisoner without a crime," I replied.

When we got to the breakfast room, it was already full. A fisticuff had ensued but the wardens intervened faster to resolve the issue. Someone had mistakenly pushed another's food. Fortunately, the victim was promised another plate, if not hell would have broken loose.

I saw criminals of all sorts. Some were chained together with others while fetters clang on their feet. They were not looking good at all. One was drooling and breathing as if her heart would jump to the floor at any time. She was a bag of bones and was shambling as a dog riddled with rabies. When I turned my face, the other way another woman who was only a shadow was coughing uncontrollably. Trickles of blood around her mouth killed the last ounce of appetite in me.

We changed places. That was when I noticed the squalid cauldrons and the dirty mugs two women were scoping the sizzling liquid from inside and pouring in cups. Once you get yours, another lady who seemed not to have had a shower ever since she came out of her mother's womb handed you a crusty piece of bread with her bare hands. The hands she had been using to pick her nose.

"The danger of contracting a stomach virus here is high," I mumbled.

"Many get treated from stomach bugs daily," Eposi corroborated.

"We are finished," Bih said.

"Most people who have family members around are better off," Eposi said.

"What do you mean?" I asked.

"They bring food to them," she said. "People can also prepare their food here."

I thought about my family. "My family is here but I can't get to them."

Eposi's face beamed.

"At 12noon when we will be allowed to see God's sunlight for an hour, I will take you to someone operating a call box business."

My face beamed. "Can we go now?"

"There are all sorts of businesses here as you will come to discover."

I stepped out of the line. I felt rejuvenated though I had no money on me to call. Eposi collected her tea and loaf of bread. She promised to give me money since I told her I had but dollars. Bih also got hers. We sat on a bench. Eposi sipped and grimaced. Bih held the murky cup to her mouth, stared at its content and held her wry face in the posture of an orangutan. I scowled at those dishing the food, pouted my lips and squeezed my eyes, feeling nauseated.

"Not even a dog can eat this," I said.

Bih shoved the bread and cup aside. A hand snatched the cup and guzzled its content almost instantly. Two hands reached out to the dry piece of bread crunching it to particles that fell on the table. They fought over the crumbs and the stronger person ate the greater share. Afterwards they fell on the crumbs on the floor like famished chicks. I looked around and was appalled that people were savoring the food like manna. Eposi nibbled her bread like a rodent. She would munch until it became liquid before she would swallow.

At 8:30am all, the male and female inmates were in the chapel. The devotion took just about thirty minutes. It did not matter whether one was a Muslim or Christian. The Catholics, Baptists, Presbyterians, and Pentecostals were all bundled up in one hall for a sermon that lacked the fervor of homilies in such crushing moments.

After that, we had fifteen minutes to meet new acquaintances. Bih, Eposi and I went to meet Larry, Pa Agbor, and Tata Banla. They too were with a friend whom they had met in the cell. He was called Cletus. All of them had jeremiads to share on how they were received, the mistreatment meted on them and how they spent the night. Unfortunately, time was not in our favor. I knew there was going to be time for them to share their individual stories and I was eagerly waiting for that.

After the chatting, we went back to our respective prisons for morning chores. We cleaned the cell and its surroundings. It was during the cleaning process that I noticed that even in prison an Anglophone is segregated against and treated as the dregs of humanity. Eposi showed Bih and me one section that barely had cartons for people to sleep on called Purgatory. She said all the people there were Anglophones. We went and greeted them, and they were so happy to meet us. Those who were assigned to clean the toilets were only Anglophones. I recalled that when the breakfast was being shared, those sharing gave more tea and larger pieces of bread to some and to others just half a cup.

"How do they know whether you're a Southern Cameroonian or not?" I asked.

"From your name tag," Eposi answered. She placed her fingers on her temples as if she had recollected something. "Oh, before I forget, remember to always come back latest 6 p.m., in short, before places become dark because you can be raped."

"By whom?" I asked.

"The wardens and prisoners are lost souls," Eposi said. "You will be shocked that some in mates are already pregnant."

When we were released at 12 noon, I could not wait. When I explained my plight to the first-class prisoner operating the telephone business, she was more than happy to assist. I dialed my husband's number with trembling hands. When he answered and noticed my quavering voice, he did not talk for a couple of seconds. He was surely overwhelmed with excitement and petrified, I thought. I was equally speechless.

He asked where I was. I was frozen. He asked again then I cooed, "Prison," and asked him to call back using the same number. My hands and feet were trembling, and I had to lean on a pole. Before I could even finish saying that he called back. I narrated my ordeal to him as he briefly told me about his frustration at the airport. He said he had just heard the most exciting news on earth because he did not know whether I was alive or dead. He further said my son had become sullen and he did not know what to tell him. He then told me he was on his way to the prison. I tried to stop him so that he should come at visitation time, he would not listen.

I was all smiles after the chat. Visitation hour that day was between 2:30 to 4pm. During lunch at 1 pm, I went to the hall where they ate just to acquaint myself with the place and perhaps meet other Southern Cameroonians to share our experiences and plight. Three giant drums draped in sooth stood on a slab like the Leshan Giant Buddha. The inmates stood in queues as they had done during breakfast. The uproar, jostling, and cursing were unbearable. I thought I could take my food and hand to someone, but the pushing and fighting was in a way I could not withstand. It was also a good distracting moment to while away time while waiting for my husband. I knew he could not come with the child since children were not permitted in prison.

I came in just when Eposi had collected hers. It was a skimpy meal made of *garri* and some exiguous soup full of fish bones. Bih also collected hers and said she wished the food could just get into her stomach without passing through her mouth. I watched her eat the food like a child forced to eat what he did not want.

Then Eposi took Bih and I around to the "market." On the way, she told us that one could get just anything from the black market, and that we needed to guard even our underwear from being stolen in broad daylight. When we got to the makeshift market, I was horrified. It was like a gambling center. A good number of the people had long tangled hair and looked unkempt. I learnt the administration had tried unsuccessfully to stop the business.

The sellers accosted everyone who came closer introducing this or that item for him or her to buy. I saw jewels, clothes, and shoes made by the prisoners. I also saw some few store items like bread, sardine, chocolate, cookies, and confections normally sold in a provision store. A scrawny wiry old man pestered me to offer any amount of money for a chain he claimed was Brazilian gold.

We stumbled on Larry and his group. He was still with his magic black pen turning it this way and that as if he wanted to cast a spell on anyone that came into contact with it. Cletus showed us where wine, whisky and drugs like cannabis and cocaine were sold. The big question on my mind was how those things got there if not being smuggled in with the help of the prison administrators. Some people were doing brisk business in the prison yard with the connivance of some top administrators. No wonder they would not like to be free. All I saw reminded me of the money exchangers in the Bible that Christ had to flog in the church.

When we got back to the cell before going to the hall where visitors were received, I waited for the administration to call me like a husband waiting to hear the news of his wife's safe delivery. I was restless and lonely in the crowded cell. Bih and Eposi, who were probably envious of me, tried to cheer me up but I was in a different world. I was restless. I will stand. Sit. Stand. Lean. When the cell's clock chimed 2 pm, my blood pressure rose to a thousand degrees. At last, I would soon be delivered. Just meeting my husband and he is telling me that my baby was kicking had transformed my heart into a keg of honey. I could feel and hear my heart drumming as if my rib cage would soon give way. I fixed my eyes on the ancient mammoth chronometer until they pooled with tears.

Time stood still as seconds ebbed to hours. I would clench my fists and close my eyes only to open them to see the time as it was before I performed the dumb act. The grits on the floor only accentuated my worries and coarseness of life ever since I landed. The people in the cell were chatting excitedly, some laughing hysterically and clasping their friend's hands. I wondered what could excite them that much. At one time, I became delusional and forgot that I was in the cell. I wanted to go out before Bih nudged me down and pointed at the iron doors with frightening bars. I brushed my back on the rugged wall and bowed my head solemnly.

When I lifted my head, inmates huddled together and blocked my view of the clock. I craned my neck to read 2:25pm. In five minutes, my worries would be history. I wondered what my husband would do immediately he saw me. Would he burst into tears? Would he go down to his knees and thank his God for saving my life? Would he lift me up, as he was fond of? Would he . . . would he . . . would he . . . I brushed all that aside and began rehearsing what I would do as soon as I met him. I would melt in his arms and drown him with hugs. Then I would kiss him as I did during our wedding in church, which sent the congregation into euphoria.

At 2:30pm, I stood and plodded towards the door wrinkling my nose. Bih and Eposi wished me well. I could see them wishing they were in my situation. As I edged myself towards the door, I did not mind the scathing remarks some of the inmates I brushed made about me. I knew obscene language was rife in a nasty place, as the one circumstances had brought me to. When I got to the door where visitors were received, it cracked open, and two guards called three inmates and took them away. After about five minutes, other guards came for more inmates. I was completely nonplussed. I did not know whether they had deliberately ignored calling me or my husband had been arrested too. About ten minutes later another set of guards came and took about fifteen inmates to go see their loved ones. My name was conspicuously absent. My joy turned to mourning.

By 3pm no one had come for me my hopes started ebbing. The guards kept coming for the prisoners but at a reduced rate. Many things went over my mind in a flash. I began to doubt even myself and started wondering whether I actually spoke with my husband, or I was dreaming. My head started pounding. I sank to the floor just by the door, sweating profusely. The inmates began raining insults on me saying an Anglophone terrorist had dropped dead. Some hovered over me making fun of me as they jeered and heaped catcalls. Some sang obscene songs bordering on the fact that I was sex starved. Bih and Eposi came to my aid and helped me to the corridor where we had passed the night.

CHAPTER THIRTEEN

On Day One of my travails, I was semi-comatose for a while though looking at places like a ghost. Bih and Eposi urged me to talk but I wouldn't say anything. My temples vibrated and my fever increased tenfold. I could not believe other family members passed before me to see their loved ones, but my husband was nowhere to be seen. I put on my thinking cap, assuring myself again and again that we have spoken to each other. Yes. That was my husband's voice. I checked the number again and it was the exact number. That number was planted on my mind. If not that we had already been quarantined in our various cells, I would have gone to the phone booth to make another call.

Eposi gave me some water to drink. It at least rejuvenated me. She handed a pack of Parle-G biscuit to me which I ravished and began scouring at places like a pig. "What must have happened to my husband?" I asked.

Eposi and Bih stared at each other in fear and looked back at me.

"Is it normal?" I asked, scratching my temple.

"Something serious might have happened," Bih said.

My heart jumped to the floor when she said that. It was logical that something fatal must have held him back. Could it be that he was in the arms of another woman when I called? Men and their schemes when women were concerned -! But he had sounded clearly without any suspicions. He was so anxious and proposed to come earlier than the time visitors were admitted to the prison. Was there a strike and taxis were not moving? But bikes were plying the streets. When we were out, I heard bikes and cars patrolling the streets. Even if he were trekking, he must have arrived before the visiting hours. "Something serious must have truly happened," I repeated. I pictured my husband in a ghastly accident where he and the driver died on the spot. I imagined the fatherless junior and myself a poor widow putting on a white satin gown at his funeral and wearing black sack clothes for years on end. My husband's funeral would take place without me. At least I should have accorded that last respect to the love of my life.

"I won't even see the remains," I mumbled. I started blaming myself for having killed him. I was the cause of his untimely death. If I didn't call him, he wouldn't have had the accident. Now he was dead and gone leaving me in prison and the child with no one to cater for. My lips pressed together in a slight grimace as I hallucinated, puffing, and huffing at the same time.

When Bih and Eposi noticed that I was drowned in thought and making some senseless comments, they shook me.

"I just meant that something uncontrollable must have held him behind," Bih said.

Eposi jiggled her foot. "Things would surely be sorted out."

"Many a time we've drawn conclusions, accused this or that person based on conspiracy theories when nothing had happened," Bih said.

After we'd eaten our dinner of plantain and cassava leaves, which I was forced to eat due to hunger, we came back to the cell and Eposi decided to tell her story so that I should not think that the world's fire was closing in on me alone. Bih too was so anxious to listen since it was therapeutic. Based on the belief that misery loved company, I decided to listen keenly. Most of the prisoners were clustered in groups chatting excitedly and I did not cease wondering what interested them so much. Eposi stretched her legs on the cartoon, placed her arms on her laps and began.

"I was fishing at the banks of River Meme while some four hefty boys were scooping sand from the bed of the river for subsistence. Suddenly, I heard some gunshots. Since the boys were so involved in the work of diving in and coming out with sand and loading it in the canoe, I alerted them. They quickly came out and we started running. Unknown to us we were running to the tiger's lair.

"The Amba Boys had overpowered La République army and killed some. The few survivors were running towards our direction and stumbled on us. They immediately tagged us as terrorists and held us captives. First, they took us to an enclosed area surrounded by thick bushes and trees and told us to sit. Immediately we warmed our buttocks on the grassy earth, they told the men to take off their clothes. I thought I was to be spared but no. I was told to take off my t-shirt and remain with my bra and trousers.

"The soldiers were determined to vent their spleen on us. They pulled our ears as if we were kids, taunting all the time. They hit our heads with gun butts. Insects on their part dealt with our flesh. First it was mosquitoes, then bees, flies, and midgets. The eight soldiers took pleasure in seeing us suffer. Soon, five other soldiers joined them. At this time, I was still hoping that they would set us free.

But when the five soldiers joined the others, we were asked to lie flat on our stomachs. Then real torture began. They hooded us and tied our hands behind and began lashing at our bare bodies with their belts. As the weapons fell on our backs, they mocked: "Speak again, Anglofou . . . Biafra you want to divide the state .

. . we will deal with you . . . *La République* is one and indivisible . . . Slaves . . ." Each phrase was followed with lashes. I screamed until I could no longer cry."

Eposi stopped speaking and began fiddling with her fingers while sobbing.

I placed my hand on her shoulder. "It is okay, my sister. Calm down."

She indicated with her fingers. "Three soldiers' gang-raped me!"

A wave of nausea hit me. "They will pay for their misdeeds one day."

Bih and I consoled her until she stopped crying and continued her harrowing experiences.

"The boys too wept out their lungs. The more they said they were innocent the more the soldiers became infuriated.

"'You can see from our clothes that we were digging sand as a means of survival,' one of the boys said.

"'Sure?' a soldier asked.

"'Yes,' he answered amidst tears.

"'Go and show us the place,' a soldier barked.

"The soldiers unhooked us and took us to the banks of River Meme where the boys showed them their tools and the fresh sand they had gathered that afternoon. I also showed them my fishing basket full of fish I had abandoned out of fright. We thought these alibis were enough reason for them to let us go. The soldiers selected two of the plump boys and told them to face the river. As soon as they turned around, they were pelted with bullets. They dropped in the river with a splash. I screamed. Four of the soldiers hooded me and dragged me to one corner and raped me in turns."

I covered my mouth in shock. Bih closed her ears popping her eyes out.

"I don't know if I am infected with HIV or any sexually transmitted disease," Eposi said. "I have neither seen any medical personnel nor been treated. How I survived those days, only God alone knows. But vengeance belongs to the Lord."

"They will never see good," I said.

"God, strike them wherever they are," Bih said.

"I will surprise you that I'm a mother of two and I don't know the whereabouts of my children and husband," Eposi said.

I adjusted myself on the cartoon and wiped my face several times. Eposi's story seems fabricated but from every indication it was the gospel truth. She was a Born Again Christian and could not fabricate such blatant lies. She was merely recounting what happened to her. "Is it true that you were raped by seven men, and you don't know the whereabouts of your family?" I asked.

She coughed and dug her tangled hair with her fingers. "Hmm my story hasn't ended."

She continued:

"After the rape, they took me back to the banks of the river. The other two boys were nowhere to be found. Your guess about their whereabouts is as good as mine. They asked me if I would like to feed the same fish I'd been feeding on. I stood confused for I was bleeding though lightly. I shook my head. They said they were taking me to a van to Yaoundé. I thought they were joking. I pleaded that I had a three-year old son and a six-year-old daughter, but all my pleas fell on deaf ears.

I was later hauled in a van. Each time the van passed by a beautiful house the driver would stop and it would be set on fire. I had never seen the darkest side of the human heart. Nearly all of Abang village was set ablaze because most of the sons and daughters of this region were abroad and have constructed mansions in the village. Before we left the village, it was already an inferno.

"I was taken to the Buyaa Principal Prison and thrown in jail where I spent a night. The condition of that hell of a place is a topic for another discussion, but I would have loved to die home than here in this foreign land where the sun may never rise.

"I didn't eat even a morsel. My complaint that I was raped meant nothing to the prison administrators who were all from La République. The next morning, we were loaded like sardine in a truck and transported to this place. It was in Buyaa that an inmate gave me a dress. Up till now I haven't heard from my husband and children. The last I heard was that the military raided our village and killed every living thing they set eyes on. And that even the few houses which seemed untouched were torched in some areas. The elderly and the sick who could not run were all burnt alive. The few survivors are in the village and those who could brave it trekked to another village.

I have also learnt that the escapees are dying in bushes and in refugee camps in Nigeria since the help promised by UNHCR is not forth coming. My two children, Emilia, and Paul," she lifted her hands, "I may never see them again. My husband was such a lovely man. Ever since I was bundled up and cast here, no one has asked me anything. I still believe I am dreaming. Wardens have attempted twice to rape me. I have been here for three good weeks," she said indicating with her fingers. "No one has said anything to me. I am sure they have forgotten about me. And I can be like this for years before the case, if at all there is any, will ever be called up."

Eposi burst into tears. "Please death have mercy and take me now," she screamed. "I want to meet my children. God have mercy."

It took our combined efforts to comfort her. Even with that she kept whimpering. Just when she had stopped sniffling, something happened that brought chaos to the little room that housed about a hundred of us.

One woman attacked another alleging she had stolen her underwear. At first, I thought it was a joke, but when the lady tore the claimed victim's breast wear, I knew it was a serious matter. She did not only end at that but lifted her skirt exposing the squalid underwear she claimed had been stolen from her. The alleged victim insisted it was hers and launched at the lady gripping her on her neck. Both tore, scratched, slapped, and beat each other as they struggled in the little space accorded them by onlookers jeering and screaming.

After they'd fought and almost rendered each other naked, the squaw told them to stop fighting. They stopped like a remote control would stop a video on the TV. She insisted she would check everyone's bag. First, she said if anyone was in keeping of the underwear, she should bring it because she was to put the mugger to shame. She waited but nobody owned up. She asked the inmates to bring their bags for her to check. They brought the bags and dumped them before her. She saw the lost item in the fifth bag she opened. The woman who was earlier accused went wild. Her supporters joined her and a fisticuff erupted. I plastered myself on the wall and crawled from there to a safe place. People jumped on others hitting and cursing. The squaw could not bring the mayhem under control. Bih, Eposi, and I managed to sneak out immediately the wardens flung the doors opened.

We got back when order was instituted. The lady who had accused an innocent woman was transferred to a different cell; even though I later heard that she served as food for the night wardens who ended up making her pregnant. When it was time to go to bed my worries began. How was I to pass the night without a word from my husband and asking after Junior? I was distraught and sat like a witch leaning on the wall and stretching my legs as far as they could go. I was inundated by gory thoughts bordering on suicide and murder. Bih and Eposi were involved in their troubles too and never cared to look at my direction. I thought of going Nawain's way by first choking a female warden to death. In that case I won't die a coward. However, I gave my plans sometime. Let it be dawn first so that I contact my husband again. I convinced myself. After that I would know the next step to take.

Hardly did we settle down when an intense heat directly from hell filled the room. Uproar seemed to have erupted in another jail. Everywhere was aglow. Then the news came that one of the buildings was afire. I thought the jail doors would be flung open but that was not the case. Instead, the wardens and soldiers mounted guards on the doors. It was only when they could not contain the heat that they ran for their safety while we fought for our survival. In seconds we brought down the steel doors. The prisoners had to use mostly sand and soil to extinguish the fire for the taps were dry. When the fire was finally put out the human casualty was incalculable. Six lives burnt beyond recognition. We got back to our cell speaking in hushed tones. I tried unsuccessfully all night to close my eyes.

CHAPTER FOURTEEN

The next day, which was DAY TWO, I didn't have the appetite to eat. After the devotion, breakfast, and morning chores I hurriedly rushed to the phone booth to make a call, but the person was not around. I came back to the cell anxious. When the opportunity arose, I rushed there again. Luckily, he was on seat, but charging his two phones placed on an upturned cigarette cartoon. A few people were also there to make one or two calls. I waited, paced up and down. At last, he gave me the phone.

When my husband answered the call, I waited for a few seconds to be sure it was his voice. My heart was beating faster. My legs were buckling slowly and my hands trembling continuously. There was no doubt it was his. He sounded excited to hear from me. I couldn't wait for him to tell me what happened. He told me to drop the call so that he could call back.

"Honey, you can't believe what happened," he said. "The roads were all blocked because His Majesty, the Supreme Head of State was travelling to Switzerland for a private visit. Oh, yesterday of all days. You know how it usually happens. The roads are blocked five hours before his departure and two hours after. You can imagine how I stood by the road fussy and sweating. I thought I could hire a bike to take me through back roads, but no biker was willing. I decided to make it on foot. Since I did not know any foot path to meander behind people's houses, I used the main road. The same road the president was to use. I chose to move mostly on people's verandas since the tiny pavements were blocked with stalls by traders.

I had already trekked about half of the journey under the scorching heat of the sun when a member of the presidential guard stopped me and handed me to a police officer for violating the injunction to stay out of the road when the His Majesty Yabi was passing. He called his subordinates who immediately hauled me on a police van. The police officer drove himself. I explained my plight to him along the way, but he wouldn't listen. I said I was not close to the road at all and that His Majesty's entourage was not even on the trail then.

"When we got to the station, I played a fast one by claiming that I was going to the hospital. Had I told them that I was going to the prison to see my wife arrested in connection with the Anglophone saga I would have been dead by now. Your situation too might have taken a different twist. Then the rest of the external family would have been on the hunt. You know La République. They would have claimed that I had a bomb to detonate when His Majesty's convoy would be passing.

"The officers asked me to take off my clothes and they pushed me in the cell. After about an hour they asked me to come out. They beat my soles until they blistered. I can't even walk. Then they seized my identity card and asked me to go and come when things were calm. I wanted to tell them that I did not understand but they pushed me out. So, I can't even come to see you because without an identity card one cannot be admitted in the prison. I would have braved the pain and come.

"Since morning I have been at commissioner Mumefoa's house. As an Anglophone, he can help secure the release of my I.D. Unfortunately; he hasn't come back since he went to work. I will go there again in the evening. That is the fate of Anglophones in this country. The stooping Yabi worshipped more than anything in this country, has caused what I am going through. If he wasn't travelling, as usual, I should have seen you yesterday. Junior is doing fine and misses you."

I was petrified when he ended the tirade. I bowed my head musing. So, I wasn't going to see and hug my husband today to get firsthand information about Junior? The worst was I didn't even know when they were to hand the document back to him. "*La République* and administrative bottlenecks," I lamented. When you come today, they will say come tomorrow and so on and so forth. The country functions like a sign post I noticed in a shop with the inscription 'come tomorrow for credit;' A tomorrow that could never come like Godot in Samuel Beckett's Play *Waiting for Godot*.

One thing was certain. If my husband had handed large chunks of money to the police officers, they wouldn't have given him his I.D. They would have collected the money and created another problem. Maybe that he should bring his First School Leaving Certificate or birth certificate or proof that the name on his birth certificate truly belongs to his mother. The only hope was to pass through the commissioner.

Though Mumefoa was a whole commissioner, he was powerless in front of his junior French-speaking counterparts. He could only act as a facilitator to give the money and collect the card. I planned to tell him next day to prepare at least 50,000 Francs CFA for that.

I got back to jail when Bih and Eposi were taking a nap. The broken door had been fixed. The heat was so unbearable that almost everyone in the cell was half naked. I squeezed myself at one corner bemoaning my fate. When we came back from dinner in the evening, Eposi asked Bih to tell us her story and how she found herself in the cell called Koussovo. She looked at us shrugged and said, "Okay."

"Hope it's not as bad as mine," Eposi said.

"Well, you listen to it and make your judgment. But all I know is that a corpse is a corpse irrespective of the cause of death."

"Come again," Eposi said.

Bih forced a smile and said; "Between a death mamba and a death boa which is stronger?"

"We are ready to hear your story. What is your story about?" I asked.

"The story is long."

"Summarize," we chorused.

Bih looked around, lowered her voice, and began.

"It was in the wee hours that about six or seven soldiers banged on our door after the peaceful march past of September 20th, 2017, that led to the death of peaceful protesters killed with helicopter gunships. I cannot claim that I didn't take part in the demonstration. It was a peaceful one and the whole village gathered at the Fon's palace who was equally for the restoration of the independence of the Anglophone - state of Ambazonians.

"So, that morning the soldiers were moving from door to door arresting young boys and girls hauling them in trucks like cattle and transporting them to the prison at Up Station to later transport to Yaoundé. It should be noted that those who were transferred to Yaoundé were those who could not afford the 50,000 to 75,000 francs FCFA bribe to secure their release.

"They dragged me from bed and handcuffed me before whisking me off to the nearest police station. There I was pushed to a dank fusty cubicle where I lived in isolation and was subjected to all forms of inhuman treatment for eight days. During this distressing period, I was treated as a beast of burden because I had to be using a bucket for my biological needs. I was also not given the chance to take a shower. I was fed with exiguous rice once a day. Each time I tried to find out why they had to keep me incommunicado, I was hushed with spanks on my jaw and back and hauled insults of being a terrorist. I gained my freedom eight days later thanks to a senior police-officer-friend of the family who secured my release since no formal charges were brought against me. But both my immediate and external family had to contribute about 20,000 francs to give to some of the police officers before I gained my freedom.

"I left the filthy cell infected with typhoid, rashes, and stomach discomfort. After regaining a bit of strength while following up with my treatment, I took a trip to Bamenda to help my sister who was blessed with a baby. I arrived Bamenda on September 29th, the eve of the All-Anglophone march on October 1st to celebrate their independence that was to take place in the two English-speaking regions.

"This peaceful demonstration became bloody as the gendarmes and military descended on the armless population with lethal weapons to stop them from exercising their civic rights. Hundreds of people including women, children, and the elderly were shot and killed at close range. The government even used more military helicopters to shoot some of the protesters whose decomposed bodies were later discovered in bushes.

"I took part in this legitimate demonstration as usual, but I was again arrested as one of several thousands that day. I was whisked off to the Up Station Gendarmerie headquarters and accused of terrorism, secession, disrespect of state institutions, arson, and incitement of violence. When I wanted to speak one gendarme tore off my dress and kicked me several times with his boots. Another officer hit my head many times with a truncheon while insulting me in French. After that he pushed me to a filthy and crowded clammy cell already suffocating with inmates.

"Before he could bang the door against me, a malodorous stench of human waste assailed my nostrils. As I groped for where to stand in the dark cell, I felt fingers touching some sacred areas on my body. That was when I knew the jail was made up of both sexes. I screamed, but that attracted more hands. When I felt some hands around my groins, instinctively I shouted that I had AIDS. Everyone recoiled. The odor from urine, feces, and sweat was unbearable. Couple with the stifling atmosphere, I almost passed out. I began crying and yelling. After a few hours in that hell, two officers came and pulled me out. Just when I was about to come out of the cell, one of them touched my buttocks and said in French that I was carrying good food. I slapped his hand."

Eposi and I laughed.

"Another gendarme gave me my torn clothes because I was just in my undergarments. When I was about putting them on, he said that since I was a terrorist, he needed to check me first. I was shocked when he started fondling my breasts in the guise of searching me. I took some steps back. When I put on the tattered shirt, he pushed me into a semi-dark cell and told me that I would "get it hot." I was in the cell all by myself. After a couple of minutes, another officer called for me that the commandant wanted to see me. From my smattering French, the commandant guessed I had surely lived in the French-speaking area and was well-informed."

Bih laughed and said she did not take her French classes in primary and secondary schools lying down.

"He told me that I would be transferred to Yaoundé, and that my release from the cell in Bafut was an error and that they had been hunting for me. This sounded strange. He asked me a series of questions warning that if I did not cooperate, he will send me to the dreaded Yaoundé prison meant for murderers and hardened criminals.

"He asked me to name the terrorist secessionist group I was linked to. I was dumfounded since I was not associating with anything of that nature. When I stood quiet, the commandant told his two subordinates to make this animal speak. The two gendarmes yanked my breasts each and pulled me closer and head-butt me a couple of times until I bled from my nostrils. Then the commandant choked me and asked me to say the truth. I repeated that I was innocent. He asked the others to undress me. Before he could even finish the statement, the dogs tore my underwear and sprayed pepper-infested liquid in my groins. It felt a trillion needles were piercing my middle kingdom.

"When I gained consciousness, I saw myself in the cell I had come from for questioning. My nipples were hurting. I also felt as if someone had attempted to rape me. Up to this day, I don't know whether I was raped, or someone had placed his fingers in my private part. I had not had the courage to tell anyone this part of my nightmare. Later in the evening, the commandant sent for me. I was literally carried to his office since I could only wobble due to torture, hunger, fatigue, and suspected rape. For fear of further anguish or being transferred to the torture chamber in Yaoundé, I told them outright lies in response to the questions they flooded me with. I said I was HIV positive and an orphan. I was vigorously whipped on my soles each time I didn't give them a favorable response. After what seemed like hours, I was taken back to the cell. There I crashed on the floor like bread doused with water. Besides the psychological traumas, I had mosquitoes and biting cold to battle with in that cage.

"I spent three days in the gendarmerie brigade undergoing unimaginable horror: eating little or nothing. On the first day I was offered cassava and no complement. I was forced to sign some papers indicating that I was liaised with some terrorists in the U.S. and Europe. I refused, and the commandant threatened to electrocute me. I insisted I could not accept what I knew nothing about. He asked his subordinates to "Show this Anglofoo something." The two gendarmes asked me to follow them and I refused and sat on the floor. They pulled me back to my cell and closed the door. There I was manhandled like a beast of burden. They kicked, slapped, and punched. I wept until I was only sniffing. They said they would spare me that day to change my mind and speak the truth.

"On my third night, one of the gendarmes came to my cell and told me to sleep with him so that he could let me escape. I lied to him that I was married and that my husband had just died of an AIDS related ailment. Some men can be so mean. Even with that he insisted that he would use a condom. I spurned his proposal.

He grabbed my breasts and wanted to kiss me, and I bit his hand. He winced and freed his hands from my breasts. That experience has left my left breast painful even till date. The next day, I was told to bring a hundred thousand francs to secure my release. I stood on the fact that I was an orphan and a widow."

"Your story parallels mine," I said.

Bih nodded. "Anglophones are guinea pigs in this country."

"How did it end, or did he rape the AIDS victim?" I asked.

"No, how dare? I was discharged from that jungle of a cell. Those three days I spent in that cell are forever etched on the dark recesses of my mind. I was not offered water for a shower, and I had only a bucket in the same room for all my bodily needs and functions. I wonder what should have happened if I had seen my menses in that semi-bunker because I menstruated the same evening I was released. It was dehumanizing because no family member could see me even though I learned that none of them had any idea of my whereabouts.

"The torture and psychological trauma I underwent during the detention toughened me. Every part of my body ached, and I had to rely on over-the-counter painkillers for a while before I could gain some relief. I also sought medical assistance at the local health center. However, my encounter with the forces of law and order surreptitiously built a lot of defiance in me. When I felt a bit better, I snuck myself to Bafut to spend some time with my parents. For fear of being recognized, since I had become a persona non-grata to the government, I disguised as an old woman and hired a motor bike to transport me to the village.

"October first the following year was the D- day set aside by Southern Cameroonians to commemorate the restoration of their independence from "La République du Cameroun." That day turned out to be an even bloodier Sunday in the English-speaking region as hundreds were again killed, hundreds maimed, and thousands abducted and dumped in dungeons across the French-speaking section of the country. Many were also declared missing on that day.

"I was caught and transported that night to Yaoundé. I am not afraid of death because everyone must die. Yabi's death will even be the worst of all deaths. Read my lips."

"These people have dealt with us," I said.

"I am a living witness," Bih said.

It is on record that days after October first's commemoration, the soldiers were still shooting indiscriminately. A bullet caught my young niece's right eye inside the house. She was playing with her siblings on their bed when a "stray" bullet hit her, shattering her face. The child was rushed to the hospital. Though she survived the onslaught, she is permanently deformed. Since then, the family has been plunged into despair and penury because of skyrocketing medical bills. It may shock you that the family had been on the run because the military has been struggling to eliminate the family."

'Why?" Eposi asked.

"You know the little girl was on the spotlight after the incident. Both the national and international media houses picked up her story and the world were awash with the horror. Some local journalists who reported the incident have been picked up already. Do you remember the old man who was interviewed on BBC radio? The military killed him the next day his interview was aired.

"I am still haunted by what happened to my little niece, and I wonder if I would ever overcome this traumatic experience. The blood that gushed out of the girl's face has been a nightmare for me to grapple with. The carnage I saw in Bamenda had shocked the very foundation of my life. I wonder whether some people were actually created by God. I had done some STD and AIDS tests to ascertain I was not raped, and I was not infected. I was however diagnosed with tuberculosis and treated. I also grapple with blood pressure ailments. I suppose it is due to the disheartening and near-death experiences I went through, the indiscriminate shootings by soldiers, and the queer face of my little niece.

"Barely three weeks after my release, I was picked up one Sunday at Ntamulung church on grounds that the leader of the coffin revolution was once my boyfriend. The soldiers who arrested me asked an eye-popping sum of a million and a half francs to let me escape to Nigeria. I could not afford a franc. I was immediately transferred to the gendarmerie headquarters in Yaoundé, where I spent months with no one asking me anything.

"I have been here for more than three months," Bih turned to me and spoke. "The day we met I was transferred from the Gendarmerie headquarters where I had been in a bunker."

"You mean to say you've been in a bunker?" I asked.

Bih bit her thin lips. "I will tell this story some other time."

"We will be more than excited to hear," I said.

She shook her tiny legs and called her name in a thick, emotion-choked voice, "Bih, Bih, Bih...I doubt if I will ever die."

CHAPTER FIFTEEN

DAY THREE came with its own peculiarities. Even if my husband were to have his ID the next day, I wouldn't have still set eyes on him. It was a Saturday and visitors were not permitted at the prison on weekends. I had to just muster courage and face my destiny. Sunday came after Saturday so I made up my mind that I will stay for two more days without meeting him. I was at least hopeful. We had spoken and he had assured me that Junior was doing great. My prayer was that he should retrieve his document for us to hug each other on Monday.

Saturday was a general cleanup day. There was no group devotion. We prayed individually. After breakfast, we engaged in keeping the place clean even though it was amusing to me. I did not understand how someone could claim to keep the bowels of a pit latrine clean. We however took everything out, scrubbed the walls and floors before sweeping and mopping. This was done in all the cells. We also off rooted the weeds around the buildings while the men cleared the bushes.

By 12:30pm we were through with the general cleaning. Some people were immediately brought to whitewash the walls of the unattended buildings. I learnt that the frantic cleanings were also because some human right investigators from abroad were to pay the prison a visit in the coming days. Words filtered around that the names of some French-speaking prisoners were earmarked to be taken out to decongest the prison during the visit. Those who were selected had to lodge in a hall at the outskirts of the city during the visit.

Since we had ample time to idle around that day, Bih, Eposi, and I looked for Larry, Pa Agbor, Tata Banla, Mekolle, and Cletus. They were so happy to see us. They took us to one lady prisoner selling beans and *puff puff* and spoiled us with food. That was my first time of eating a real meal after many days. We ate and chatted on frivolities. No one could believe that we had found ourselves in the worst prison in the world.

Tata Banla burped, as we ate, and said, "I wish I had some kola-nuts and palm wine to push this heavy meal down. I wonder how my palm bush looks like now."

My lips trembled. "Were you a tapper?"

"Hmm my daughter,' he slapped his chest, "I was the best palm wine tapper in *Ngongbaa* and beyond. Haven't you heard about Tata Banla's wine? Not that thing mixed with saccharine and sold to people to pollute their stomachs with. I was coming back from the palm bush before some fierce-looking men in uniform kidnapped me."

"Really?" Bih and Eposi asked at once.

"Yes. I asked the soldiers what they were abducting an old man for, but they didn't care. They drank all the wine I'd collected that fateful day taunting me as they did so. Imagine my grandchildren asking me to kneel and lift both of my hands as if I was an infant.

"After glugging the two jugs of palm wine, they broke the containers and shattered my bicycle in pieces as if it was a weapon of mass destruction. They also destroyed my tapping machete and tools. One pulled my cap and landed a slap on my bald head"

We cringed and covered our faces.

"This is what they did to me," he continued. "Then they pulled me up and began pushing me from one end to the other. The worst part was that they were speaking in French—a language I knew nothing about. Only one of them could speak some smattering pidgin. He said I should show them the terrorists that were in my keeping. When I insisted that I was innocent, they beat my soles with some thick rubber. Each blow fell on my feet like a bag of cement.

"Then they asked me to follow them. I thought they wanted to take me to my compound so that I could prove my innocence, but they rather took me to a military truck and threw me inside like an animal. Even animals are treated nowadays with dignity. I pleaded that I was asthmatic and suffered from arthritis. They ignored my pleas.

"On the truck I met some five boys. Their hands were tied behind. They kept begging that they were university students who have come home because the insurrections have caused schools to close, but it appeared there was wax in the ears of the soldiers. We arrived Bamenda late that night. The soldiers parked the truck in front of the governor's office which was heavily guarded. We had to pass the night in it. Anyone who knows the biting cold at Up Station can testify. Since I didn't develop pneumonia or die that day, I think I will only die when God calls me.

"The next day the military collected more boys from the jail and bundled us behind the truck. I can remember my primary school history textbook by S.N. Tita. It had the picture of slaves huddled together like timber in a ship. That was how we drove to Yaoundé. We were at the Gendarmerie Headquarters in Melen for a month before being transported here.

"The wickedness I saw there can be compared to none. We were about twenty of us in a bunker. The human heart is wicked, and full of devilry. If someone had told me that a human being with blood like this," he pinched the vein of his arm, "could do this to another I would have said it is a big lie because even Satan himself is sometimes merciful. We were in the bunker for two days without water or food."

"The disgusting realities at SED – *Gendarmerie Nationale* caused by Yabi's killer squad are unimaginable. We were locked up in chains and handcuffs in a darn basement and forced to sleep on an ice-cold floor. Water was thrown on the floor to wet the stinking lean mattresses a few inmates had. We were accorded the opportunity once a day to go out to worship the image of His Majesty Yabi in one hall. We had no access to God's sunlight except the electric light that almost destroyed my eyes.

"Once we came back from kneeling before the picture that filled the entire wall, we were rendered bare bodied again and the iron door banged behind us. We were deprived of sleep and had a shower after every two weeks. We had no toothbrushes, no toilet paper, and no soap. The Gendarmerie Headquarters is hell incarnate.

"We have suffered. We were tortured daily with planks until some pooped in their underwear. Some soldiers used wax from lighted candle to burn our genitals after being beaten with electrical cables, and machetes. Sometimes, they used pincers on our scrotum and armpit. A day did not pass by without them threatening to execute us. I wish they had. On such days, we were blindfolded and taken out and asked to say our final prayer. By the time they brought us back we were smeared with our poop and urine due to extreme torture."

I flinched and said, "Eposi do you hear that? Repulsive."

Tata Banla resumed.

"We were held incommunicado with no access to a family member, lawyer, or pastor. I will never forget how Amabo and Ebini shackled and handcuffed together were tortured morning and evening. They were so beaten on the soles of their feet with machetes dipped in water that they could not walk. On some days they were beaten with iron rods, sticks, cables to make the excruciating pain more biting and gruesome. After each session of torture, they were asked to jog, at times blindfolded for days, and the lights turned off for days in their bunker."

"Why were they singled out?" I asked.

"I learnt that they hoisted the Ambazonian flag in front of a police station in Batibo."

"What finally happened to them?" Larry asked while playing with his pen.

Tears gushed out of Tata Banla's eyes. "They did not make it."
Bih sniffled.

"The day we were to be transported here, I told them not to bother. I said it was needless because I wanted to die, and I meant it. They had fettered and bundled me like a stubborn heifer and thrown me on the floor of the truck before I found myself here."

We sat taciturn which was occasionally broken by a sniffle.

CHAPTER SIXTEEN

On Sunday, which was DAY FOUR, we went to church in the prison yard. The Christians were bundled together, irrespective of denomination, under one roof—a makeshift shed with a tarpaulin full of holes as roof. The Muslims were excluded since they worshipped on Friday. In my days in the dreaded prison and even after, I kept wondering why the administration would jumble the Christians and Muslims for morning devotion only to separate them on Fridays and Sundays. I saw the bringing of both religions together as a potential keg of gun powder and fire.

Since we were so many, some of the congregants had to stand for lack of seats. I was fortunate to have secured a seat in front since I'd come early. Even though the first row of seats was reserved for the V.I.P.'s the seats were essentially the same. It was quite humbling for me to sit closer to top notch politicians in the guise of ministers whom I'd never seen in real life who were now prisoners. Amongst the dignitaries attending the church service were former ministers like the prime minister, the minister of defense, the Minister of Finance, the Minister of Livestock, Fisheries, and Animal Husbandry, the Minister of Communication, the Minister of Higher Education, the General Manager of the National Radio and Television, and the General Manager of Aviation. Almost every ministry was represented, and I could understand why someone had said that the prison was a full cabinet except for a head of state. People had prophesied that if Yabi lived a bit longer, he would face the International Criminal Court of Justice.

I was distracted at the beginning of the church service because of the presence of those onetime movers and shakers of the state who hitherto thought they were unshakeable. They were so wicked that they did not make the prisons at least comfortable for human habitation. Now it was their domicile. The Yaoundé maximum security prison that was designed to house 800 inmates was stifling more than 10,000 prisoners. The former prime minister looked pale and disoriented, and drooled all the time he was in church. The other cabinet members were not looking any better. They sat like wizards and as if they would not see the next day. They all hunched on their seats as if they were on a burial ground to pay their last respects to a dear friend. Their hands either supported their sunken chin or were clasped in between their laps.

The no-nonsense prelate, Archbishop Simon Nyuyki, preached a brief and powerful homily entitled "Good Deeds Last Forever." He drew his inspiration from Proverbs 29:1-2 which he read again and again: (1) *He, that being often reproved hardeneth his neck, shall suddenly be destroyed, and that without remedy. (2) When the righteous are in authority, the people rejoice: but when the wicked beareth rule, the people mourn."*

He told a cautionary tale about a man whose name was "Do Good, Do-am For Yourself; Do Bad, Do-am For Yourself." He said the man was so kind and selfless that he was hated by the people around him. One of them detested him so much that he gave him poisoned bananas. Since he wasn't hungry, he didn't eat them. On returning home, he met the same man's children who had given him the fruits. They complained of hunger, and he gave them the bananas. After eating the bananas, they developed acute gripes. Their parents asked them what they ate when they returned home. "Do Good Do-am For Yourself gave us some bananas," one of them said.

"I am finished," their father exclaimed.

He shook the children scolding them for eating things given by strangers, but it was too late. Before he could get to the hospital with them for urgent medical attention, they had both given up the ghost.

"Those who live by the sword shall die by it," the priest said.

He put his homiletics lessons into practice as he stared at the congregation waiting for his message to sink. "Those who live by the sword shall die by the sword," he repeated as he paced in front of the large crowd, his black cassock with pink and white stripes blown by the wind. He warned those in power who made life difficult for the common man hoping they will continue to wine and dine till their last day on earth. He said rain fell on the crops of Christians and the heathens and that airplane disasters do not know first-class or second-class seats.

"Build good roads, schools, and hospitals for all and sundry for you never know when you will need them. The seeds you plant today are what you will harvest tomorrow. Be a ladder to your fellow man. One good turn deserves another," he concluded.

The crowd was dead silent. I lifted my head and saw the men of timber and caliber mortified and jittery. The homily ended with a communion service. To my chagrin all the ex-ministers who had connived with His Majesty Yabi to destroy the nation also partook of the Holy Table. They had sung his praises and made the common man suffer to please the tyrant, but he turned around and threw them in dungeons.

I felt for them, especially those who'd eaten the communion without repentance for they were heaping God's curse upon themselves and their generations.

After the church service, I called my husband who said he was with Commissioner Mumefoa and that I should call the next day. Larry, Tata Banla, and Pa Agbor took Bih, Eposi, and me to a stall where one of the prisoners sold soft drinks. Each of us took a bottle of Fanta soda and began nursing to drown our frustration. Immediately we took our first sips, Tata Banla turned to Pa Agbor and asked him to share his experiences about his adoption and eventual transportation to Yaoundé.

Pa Agbor sipped once more as he held the bottle with his clogged gnarled knobby fingers. He thrust the entire neck of the bottle in his scanty mouth before dropping it on the table with a thud. The old man had lost all his canines and a few molars making his mouth look like a flabby balloon. He seemed to suffer from Parkinson syndrome because he was shaking all the time. He used his right hand to wipe his bald head that had some wiry white hairs before sitting contemplatively as if he'd forgotten what he'd been asked.

"What happened to you Pa?" I asked.

He evinced a cadaverous smile, licked his cracked lips and said, "It all happened one afternoon when I did not go to my cocoa farm. My hernia and backache were so terrible that day that I could not even get up from bed. My wives and children had gone to trim the dry twigs from the cocoa plants when the devils in the name of soldiers pounced on my homestead."

"How many wives and children do you have, Pa," I asked.

"Two wives and eleven children."

Larry curbed his hand around his mouth. "Eleven children!"

"Yes. My late father had sixteen children. If two did not die in their infancy, they would have been eighteen. Ha my children, that was in those days when the world was a good place. Now you can't see eye to eye with your neighbor."

I was curious. "What happened on that day?"

"I was in bed groaning. Suddenly, I heard some stampede like the usual military booths when soldiers are on parade. It seemed as if I was dreaming because in as much as the soldiers have committed a lot of atrocities in my village by killing people and burning houses, they've never encroached in the hinterlands where I perched with my family. I lay still in bed listening as the noise grew louder. Soon they were in my homestead. I felt my temple throbbing because of late the men in uniform have burnt the elderly and the sick alive in their homes. Amongst those burnt alive that day were two cripples and a madman. The memory of the women and children killed in the Northern Zone and burnt in a house were still fresh in my mind too. I feared for the worst, the manner of death and the fact that I may not see my family.

"I heard two gunshots coming from the courtyard. One of the soldiers shouted in pidgin that if there was any Amba fighter in the houses they should come out at once and surrender. When no one came out, I heard a bang on my first wife's door. Then on my second wife's door. I crawled under my bed. After a couple of minutes, it was unbearably hot. I crept out and my ears were pestered by a crackling flame. I ran out of the house only to meet the two houses roaring ablaze. One of the soldiers had just poured fuel on the roof of my house and was trying to get fire from one of my wife's houses to set it ablaze too. I stood catatonic watching all I've worked for crumble before my eyes in seconds."

I could not contain the horror. Bih sniffled.

"You mean to say this thing happened before your very eyes?" I asked.

"Let *Obasinjom* strike me dead if I am telling a lie," Pa Agbor said. "Hmm they said I was lucky to have run out because I would have been burnt alive. I told them about my fragile health and my large family, but no one listened. I was handcuffed like a bandit and dragged to a waiting van while my earthly labors were being consumed by sputtering flames.

We drove to the Abang abandoned airport where some thirty young men without clothes except underwear sat on their buttocks at the esplanade waiting hopelessly. We were hauled to the waiting military plane which took off immediately. Somewhere in the air the soldiers began throwing some of the young men out of the plane. I died and resurrected."

Bih ran away and came back. I closed my eyes and ears. When I opened them, Pa Agbor continued in the same grim jocularly manner.

"Before we got to Yaoundé only twenty youths out of the thirty were left. We were transported to the gendarmerie headquarters and later to the police headquarters for identification formalities and questioning. Later, a heavily guarded army truck drove us to the outskirts of the city to a prison yard where we spent two months before I was transferred here."

"Why are they transferring some people here and leaving others?" I blurted out my feelings.

Pa Agbor looked at Tata Banla and both looked at Eposi. No one responded. He groped for his drink with his trembling hands. Took a sip and kept it back.

"Have your wives and children been contacted?" I asked again.

"Pa Agbor bowed his head. "The last I heard was that the soldiers shot my first son. I have not been charged for any crime. I have not yet gone to court. My family is in the bush. That is all I can say. Death you are wicked. Cruel. I've begged many times for you to take me. But no! Our people say that dry leaves fall first. Heartless and blind death is determined to go only for the young people."

He burst into tears. It was painful seeing a man as old as my father weep. Tata Banla placed his hand on his shoulder and told him to be courageous and that God would fight the Southern Cameroonian battle.

"These people are despicably villainous," Larry blurted.

After we were done with our drinks, we moved around the prison yard. Larry's little black pen gripped in-between his fingers. The clearing or so-called clean-up campaign seemed to have changed nothing. The gutters and potholes were fraught with standing water full of algae, mosquitoes, and frogs. Almost all the buildings had sewage seeping behind them. No one seemed to care about the continuous seepage. There was no building without a major issue needing urgent repairs ranging from cracked walls, falling roofs, to leaning pillars. I shook my head when I saw the time bombs.

In the discovery mission, one thing caught my interest. Larry was manipulating his pen throughout. I just kept wondering why a grown up would be doodling with a short pen as if he were a kid. I attempted asking him what was so particular about the pen but hesitated.

We later got to our cells enervated with no energy to even tell stories. I sat on my cartoon waiting for dawn so as to contact my husband about the recuperation of his I.D.

CHAPTER SEVENTEEN

On DAY FIVE, dark clouds hung in the air preventing the sun from rising and seeping its vibrant rays through the many tiny windows high above on the walls of the cell like the devil's eyes. Though, it was not the peak of the rainy season, the thick clouds continued to gather above the sky in a threatening and dicey manner. The usual morning hullabaloo characterized by weird laughter and sadness was absent.

Before we could step out for the morning devotion the news was on everyone's lips. Four wardens had raped two female inmates to death. In one of the men's cells, two inmates had jointly choked another to his demise. The news was scary, and I was not myself when I stepped out.

After the usual morning devotion, I ran to the call box operator hoping that by some luck he would be there. The sun had begun to send its rays to take away the night's dew and warm the city. But since he was a prisoner too, he wasn't there yet. I lingered around until after breakfast and normal prison chores before getting there.

I got in touch with my husband who said Commissioner Mumefoa told him to come in the evening to his house to collect the card. He said he had spent 75,000 francs FCFA to resolve the issue. He assured me that Junior was doing fine and that he hoped to see me the next day.

Just when I dropped the call Larry came too to contact someone via phone. He said he had called a number of relations before, but they were scared to travel from the English-speaking region to the Francophone area. They cited cases of arbitrary arrests, torture, incarceration, and swindling of huge chunks of money by French-speaking militia while on transit. I later gathered that it was all true. Anglophones were constantly being harassed and money extorted from them. Those visitors who braved it and got to the prison were either incarcerated or tortured and asked to pay for their freedom. The lucky ones were sent away for not being able to communicate in French.

"I think they are right," I said. "Travelling from the Northern or Southern Zone to the Francophone area is synonymous with Muslims entering some countries in the western world. The way the security officers scrutinized the English-speaking citizens was alarming."

"Don't you think it would have been better for us to go our separate ways since they are the ones who broke away from the federation in 1972?"

I pouted. "These people cannot let us go. Remember our potential."

"You mean the natural resources?"

"Yes. We have the oil, the timber, the touristic sites, the fertile soil, and what have you?"

"It was really unfortunate that our forefathers rallied us to join these people," Larry said. Everything about them is weird. Here we are prisoners without being tried."

Larry chuckled. "There is hope. Our people have risen. Let them kill us all. The idea will live to fight until freedom comes."

"I strongly believe so."

"I have been planning to ask you about your experience in your own prison."

Larry shook his head. "Let me make this call, and then we can talk about it."

114

He dialed the number several times and complained that the person was not picking up the call. He tried four other numbers in Bamenda, Ndop, Limbe and Tiko with no success. He then recalled that their phones could be ringing in the air as the government cut off internet access from the two English-speaking regions for three months and counting. He tried another number and the person answered immediately in Douala. He said he would come by Friday since he was in a Francophone zone. Larry and I traipsed to a shed under a shrub and sat down. He showed me the welts on his legs and wrists caused by chains from the previous incarceration. I flinched as I felt the spots with my finger.

"How has it been in your cell?" I asked.

He shrugged his shoulders. "Hell on earth."

"You don't mean it."

"When I got in the first day, I thought I would not see the next second. Immediately the door was flung open, a wave of heat slammed me to the floor. The place was well lit, and people were coughing from all the corners. I struggled to my feet sweating all over my body. As I groped my way in, I noticed it was jammed to capacity and I literally threaded on people's feet as I squeezed myself to find a place to stand. The inmates pinched me as I groped my way to a place where I could at least stand without rubbing my body on someone. The heat, bad breath, and the toilet made matters worse. I looked around hoping to see a means of escape. There was none. The murky ceiling was far above the sky; dripping continually."

"About how many of you were in that cell?" I asked. I wanted to say I hope he hadn't contracted tuberculosis but held my breath.

"Not less than two hundred. What my eyes saw there—" Larry bit his lips and groped for where to place his hand. "I saw

115

bones in the name of humans; these can't come for devotion, breakfast, and lunch. These were hardened criminals who have murdered countless times and buried some alive. They were in chains."

"And those were the people they sent you to be with?"

"What do you want me to say? Rashes, scabies, ringworm, lice, and ticks have eaten them until there is nothing left. I could count the bones on their ribs."

Larry spat behind him somewhere in the variegated grass. "I met two living corpses. The chains have so chopped off their ankles that the bones on their legs were clearly out, maggots swirling and pus oozing. They have gone through so much pain that they have lost the sense of feeling. Some of the prisoners were blind due to so much exposure to light."

"Did you use the toilet?"

"No, but I saw it since the door to it had been destroyed. There was human waste everywhere because the drainage was bad."

"How did you sleep?"

"Miracles do happen. I was wondering how I was going to sleep and how the people do sleep when one of the inmates landed a slap on my back. I jerked sideways and stumbled on someone who pushed another causing all the inmates to feel the wave of the impact. The inmates started rioting. This brought in some prison administrators and the cell was decongested. I was lucky to be amongst those taken out to another cell."

"Hope this one was better."

He nodded. "Even though all compartments in hell are the same." He cleared his throat. "There was some relief in this. I don't know the criterion that was used. All I know is that God above is alive. Immediately I was told to move to the other side while others were sent back, I heaved a sigh of relief." He began playing with his short pen.

"You and this pen," I said, "Like one's legs; it can't be separated from you."

He cachinnated. "Well, if you must know, it's not an ordinary pen. It's actually a digital camera and can take videos too."

I seized it and he snatched it from me. "You don't mean it."

"Please, don't destroy it," he cried. "It's loaded with tons of information and the international community is awash with what is going on. The pen has a chip which is connected to a friend's laptop in the U.K."

"I respect you," I said. "It's good to bow to superior intellect."

"His Majesty Yabi and his cabinet are in deep shit," he hissed. "Wait and see."

"Good news from you. It's so comforting," I screamed. "People are not sleeping."

"The Red Cross, Human Rights, and Transparency International, and the International Criminal Court have their noses in *La République*."

"I'm glad. So, you were in a semi heaven as compared to your previous cell?"

"The new cell had less inmates. To crown it all, Tata Banla and Pa Agbor were in this cell."

I stretched. "Miracle indeed. So, were you able to sleep comfortably?"

"Where, my sister? Can any man in the bed of an ocean be comfortable? At least people took turns in this cell to sleep; unlike the previous one called 'Lucifer's Chamber One' where there was no way to lie down at all."

"Ha. Strange name indeed. What is the present one called?" I was inquisitive.

"The Gate to Hell."

"Are these not satanic names?"

"What can I say? Our people used to say that someone who has AIDS needs not fear other venereal diseases. About two people in The Gate to Hell had telephones and four had radios. That was our bond with the outside world. We could listen to local news and foreign news which we listened to often, especially VOA and BBC."

I swayed on my feet. "You earlier said people took turns to sleep in The Gate...hmmm I won't complete that," I said. "How did you do that? And were there beds?"

"You arrange with someone who gets to sleep for four hours on a bare mattress as thin as a razor blade. Then he gets up and you sleep too. You pay 500 francs FCFA to sleep on a mattress."

"The earlier we leave this place, the better."

"I have a strong feeling that something will happen. As they say, a clear conscience need not fear."

"I hope so, especially now that the sit-tight president's status has waxed and waned."

We separated, hoping to see each other the next day and praying fervently for a miracle to happen so that we would be released as soon as possible. I had not even plodded up to six meters when I heard a scuffle. Behold a prison guard had gripped Larry on the collar as if he'd been caught raping the man's wife. He threw his biro to me, and I caught it and ran towards the two men, but before I could get there another prison guard had joined his colleague to wrestle Larry down. The guards kept hollering that he was a notorious terrorist as they rained punches on Larry's face. They said he needed to be fettered and isolated. He overpowered the two men as they scampered in different directions.

The scene had attracted more prison guards and two soldiers. As if in a gun-shooting exercise, one of the trigger-happy soldiers pulled his gun. Two bullets landed on Larry's chest. He dropped to the ground like a piece of wood. Without any movement Larry was gone, his eyes wide open and blood trickling out of his mouth. The others congratulated the soldier on being an excellent marksman. This was accompanied by slurs on Larry's lifeless body.

I froze momentarily. When I regained consciousness, my buttocks were on the ground. I was grimacing and wanting to look away but was unable to take my eyes off the frozen body. I covered my mouth with my palms as tears gushed out of my eyes. I tried to stand but the heavy feeling in my stomach could not permit me to. I pressed my hands against my ears. Time seemed to standstill. I wished it was not true. Within minutes before my very eyes Larry's remains were dumped in a human bag and taken away. I swallowed rapidly to dispel a thick ache in my throat.

One of the guards shouted that I should leave. I stood but my legs buckled. A kick on my buttocks brought me back to my senses. I pressed my hand against my breastbone and tried to close my eyes but was unable. I stumbled a few steps and stood. Petrified.

"Go!" a voice thundered. I took a deep breath to try and regain control of my emotions.

When I got to my cell, Eposi was deep in meditation. Bih was taking a nap. I sat quietly beside them. After she finished praying, she began humming in a very low tone—a song my husband was fond of singing when in trouble:

Paul and Silas
They Prayed
They sang
The Holy Ghost
Came down.

I started moving my lips to the rhythm of the song. When she opened her eyes, I told her the shocking and brutal killing of Larry. She tried twice to speak but her words dried up in midsentence. Then she burst into tears. Bih woke up and joined us.

At 6 p.m. the prison went into such a frenzy that the officials could not contain the jubilation. They asked everyone to go out. What had filtered from the 6 p.m. news was on everyone's lips. The pressure on His Majesty Yabi from the international community influenced by Larry's videos and pictures on the despicable state of the prison finally bore fruit. Yabi had signed a decree for anyone connected to the Anglophone uprising to be released with immediate effect. News too was filtering in that an inclusive dialogue to solve the Anglophone Problem would take place.

The euphoria in the prison yard was deafening. People embraced each other, beat their chests, and jumped on walls. Others climbed on trees. Some plucked tree branches and waved them around as they sang. Yet others were singing, beating utensils and anything they could lay hands on.

The mouths of others soon to be released went slack. Then they burst into paroxysms of laughter as they stood in groups, not believing what had just happened. A few took some frantic steps away from the group only to turn around and come back after a couple of meters; their voices wondering aloud, "I can't believe it. Yabi may be under the influence of opium." In spite of the doubts expressed by some, one could still see wide smiles on their faces.

I just could not hold back the tears of joy that kept rolling down my cheeks as I experienced spells of adrenaline spikes. I staggered towards Bih and Eposi and melted in their arms. We wished Larry were with us. Bih was blinking rapidly and staring into space afterwards. I could see her slit eyes sparkle and gleam.

She pressed her palms to the sides of her cheeks, squealing dramatically.

Eposi's lips parted. "Thank you, Jesus. Thank you, Jesus," I heard her saying. She danced frantically around and buckled on her knees, praising God.

I stood in a stiff posture, the sound of blood rushing in my ears. I was eager to share the experience with my family members and anyone who cared to listen, but unfortunately, they were not around. My heartbeat was racing, and I was experiencing shortness of breath. I clasped my hands and pressed them tightly on my chest. I was awestruck; hypnotized. I felt my insides vibrating.

At last, I would be united with my family. No news had ever dazzled me before. I could sense my shoulders dropping and my heart rate picking up. I was caged in the jaws of death and could not wait for dawn. The last verse of the Bible echoed in me. I transmuted it to fit my situation. "Even so, come, Tuesday. Come with my husband and son," I muttered as I waited for DAY SIX which was to be the end of my tale.

GLOSSARY

Tuhkuni: mashed potatoes and beans

Obasinjom: "God's medicine", - the strongest of the medicines among the Ejagham people of Cameroon with powers of prophecy. It can strike one dead or with a disease if they falsely swear by it. Invoking it means one is speaking the truth and nothing but the truth.

WADA: Wum Area Development Authority

UNVDA: Upper Noun Valley Development Authority

PWD: Public Works Department

MIDENO: Mission de Développement du Nord Ouest (French acronym for North West Development Authority)

MIDEVIV: Mission de Développement des Vivres du Cameroun (French acronym for Food Crop Development Authority).

POWERCAM: West Cameroon Electricity Corporation

CAMEROON BANK: Farmers' Bank

Review Requested:

We'd like to know if you enjoyed the book.
Please consider leaving a review on the platform
from which you purchased the book.

9 781682 358382